# Now & Then

Cadence James

# Synopsis

I n the enticing sequel, *Now & Then*, the vibrant city lights of Las Vegas set the stage for a night of unexpected revelations and heartfelt promises. After a wild evening filled with laughter, love, and a touch of intoxicated spontaneity, the couples find themselves reliving the aftermath of experiences that change their lives forever.

Bleu, ever the romantic, is determined to make Mila's dreams come true. With Bleu's love as her anchor, Mila finds herself at a crossroads torn between fear and faith, past and possibility.

In *Now & Then*, Mila and Bleu must embrace vulnerability, passion, and faith in love to discover what truly matters and decide whether to cling to the comfort of what was or boldly step into the unknown possibilities of what could be.

# Dedication

*Mommy, this is for you. xoxo*

# Playlists

Headphones? Check. Wine? Check. Now get comfy and vibe out.

**Apple**
https://music.apple.com/us/playlist/now-then/pl.u-xl yNJRYukoVKYE

**Spotify**
https://open.spotify.com/playlist/0cbeYsZscbsqc69A LzyDEx

# Contents

# Author's Note

What's up, good people? Thank you for rockin' with me and the beautiful souls of Cadence. This sequel/finale made its way to you way later than I planned, but I'm grateful you're here for the ride. This story is meant to be experienced after reading Ignited On The Fourth: Seduction in Red, White, and Blue, where the heart, history, and foundation of this world begin. I hope you enjoy diving back into this love, this town, and this journey right along with me.

This novel includes explicit language, steamy sexual content, and subjects that may be triggering or difficult for some readers. Some triggers may include but not be limited to:

- Lupus flare-ups

- Abandonment

- High risk pregnancy

- Phase of Life events

Keep in mind that we all move through life differently. Something that seems unlikely or unrelatable to you may be someone else's everyday life. And while this story draws from many real emotions and experiences, it remains a work of fiction.

Now, with all the housekeeping out of the way, LET'S GET IT! ENJOY!!

# Glossary

To help you step fully into the world of ***Now &***
***Then***, the following glossary offers the correct pro-
nunciations, meanings, and cultural notes behind the
names, places, and terms used throughout the story. Cadence is rich with history, lineage, and layered identities,
and this guide is here to make your reading experience
smoother, deeper, and even more enjoyable. Feel free to
reference it at any time as you journey through the pages.

**Mila** – (Mee-Lah), MiMi, Mi
**JaCaryous** – (Jah-Car-Ree-Us), Bleu, JP, Jay
**Zariah**, Zariah Jackson - (Zah-Ree-Yuh), ZiZi, Zi
**Redd** - Redd Jackson
**Cara** - Cara Love (Carr-Ruh), CiCi, Ci
**Whyte** - Weston William Whyte
**JJ** - John Jacob Patrick, Bleu's Brother
**Ephraim** – (Eff-fry-am), Pops
**LB** or line brother
**Frat** or fraternity brother
**Sorors** or sorority sisters
**Poiré** – (Pour)
**Corqué** – (Cork)
**Sommé** – (soh-MAY)
**Sémillon** – (SEH-mee-yawn)
**Zoëra** – (Zoy-rah)

**Vertrees** – (Ver-treece)
**Naya** – (Nay-yah)
**Jessinia** – (Yah-sin-knee-yah)
**Nana** – (Nannah like Hannah)
**Jeaux** – (Joy)
**Flëur** – (Flurr)

# Then...

# Prologue

# Chapter 1
# MILA

*J*uly *4th*...

Redd is preening and strutting around like a peacock ever since he gathered his clues in the scavenger hunt and learned that Zi is pregnant. Her, not so much so, and I'm lowkey concerned. I make a mental note to check-in with her.

Whyte and Cara are friendly enough. The tension seems to have melted between them for the most part.

And Bleu. My man, my man, my man. It sounds funny saying that and looking over at him, knowing that this fine specimen of a man wants me. If it were left up to him, we'd be married before midnight. I wish I was as secure as he is in this relationship. And it's nothing he's done, it's all me and my crazy insecurities.

We all make our way back to the bar where Bleu surprised me with an in-person karaoke performance by thee *Heyoka Jones,* in the flesh, performing my favorite song of hers, Teena Marie's *"Out On A Limb."* I'm straight fangirling! She even called me up on the stage to sing with her! Talk about thanking him with some of the best brain he has ever had, I did that! He could barely move. I tried to suck his ancestor's souls through his dick.

Grinning, I lead Bleu from his office to the bar area where the others are talking. "Where y'all been? Ooooo Mi, you look like you been up to no good," Cara teases, laughing.

"Oh, I've been good, ain't it, Bae?" Laughing, I lean into him.

Whyte looks up from his phone and announces, "Aye, so my boy is spinning at this dope ass spot in Vegas. He just gave me six VIP passes and a few suites at the Venetian for the next two nights. If we leave now, go home and pack, we should be able to find commercial flights for tonight. We are three hours ahead so that gives us plenty of time."

"I can check with one of my colleagues and see if his G5 is available for tonight, giving us time to find flights back if necessary." Cara types away on her phone.

"Bet," Whyte replies.

"That's whassup, Ci," Bleu agrees.

"Oh, you got energy for that, Bleu?" I quirk my eyebrows at him, smirking. He blushes but doesn't answer me.

"Besides, I do have some business to conduct while I'm there. Two birds, one stone." She adds, walking away. Doubling back, "Bleu, I have some home options for you to take a look at on the plane." She breezes out of the door, not waiting for an answer from him.

Bleu turns to look at me, questioning if I want to go. I immediately look away. I don't care for Vegas but don't want to spoil his fun.

"Mrs. Patrick, you good?"

"I mean.... If you want to, we can." I reply.

He immediately comes to me and lifts my face upward to search my eyes. With one look, he questions, "Do you want to go? What's wrong?" And ends with, "Whatever you want to do, I'm fine."

"Sure, why not? What's the worst that can happen? We act like we're in a rom-com and get married?" I acquiesce, laughing, pulling out of his grasp.

Redd, Whyte, and Bleu look at each other and bust out laughing.

Redd looks at me and shakes his head, still laughing as he and Zariah leave.

Whyte touches my shoulder, "Little one, one day you are going to learn." And walks away.

"Say less, Mrs. P." Bleu gives me a brief kiss on the lips and grabs my hand, leading us out the door.

"Come on, baby, so we can pack."

"I hate packing." I complain.

"You won't be wearing much of anything, anyway. So don't bother." He whispers in my ear.

"Whyyyy are you like this, JaCaryous?" I ask him while getting into his car.

*＊＊

Hours later, I swear it was like a fast forward motion of flying, checking into the hotel, showering, changing clothes, drinking, laughing, smoking, and partying. Where are we? Where are my clothes?

My head is so fuzzy. I stumble into the bathroom. Finally, sitting on the toilet, I'm holding onto the sink next to me so I don't fall, with just my heels on.

The fuck? I'm trying to recall the nights events.

"Think Mila think," I whisper to myself.

There were colored lights in the dark club, singing, dancing, and drinking. And...smoking. Yes! That shit is legal here. Cara's ass had me trying some sweet treat. Zariah. *Where is Zariah? She's pregnant. Right? Did I even see Redd?*

*Fuuuuuucccckkk! What did Cara give me? Bleu. Where is he?* Ima punch his ass in the throat. He kept blowing that shit in my mouth. None of these niggas can be trusted.

"Why am I naked with just these shoes on? Who am I right now?" I whisper, still holding onto the sink, slowly looking down because the room is spinning.

I vaguely remember leaving the club. It was soooo many lights! We were on the strip, in a car. I think. Things were moving fast and then we weren't. Then it was bright and more lights.

Whyte. Whyte was so lit, he just kept grinning and hugging me, holding mine and Cara's hands. *Where is she?*

Wait a fucking minute! I look down at my hand and the memories hit me like Tyson did Frazier in that 30 second knock out fight.

*"BLEU!!!!"*

# Now...

# *Chapter 2*

# BLEU

**V**egas, July 5th, Next Morning

"Maaaannnnn. Whaddup, Frat?" I dap my boys, Whyte and Redd, up as I walk into the hotel restaurant.

Kissing Zariah, Redd's wife, on the cheek, "Hey, Love."

"Morning. Where's Mila?" she asks.

"She was still sleep when I left. I want to have some food ready for her when she wakes up. I know she's hung over after the night we had."

"Whyte just started telling us about last night. Y'all cut up. Thank you, baby." She kisses

Redd as he sets a plate of food in front of her.

"Anything for the love of my life and mother of my child. You need anything else, babe?"

"Nah, this is way too-"

"JaCaryous Kristoff Patrick!!"

Wide-eyed, my stomach drops. That voice! That sound! Like nails on a chalkboard over a choir of congested cats.

I turn slowly in the direction of the ear-splitting noise and saw Anise.

The bane of my existence comes barreling across the dining room in a red sequin dress that looks like unraveling bandages and stripper-borrowed platform heels. Hair down to her ass, tangled and fake, lashes so heavy, she can barely open her eyes. Which has got to be a lie because she scoped my ass out across a crowded room.

She is not attractive to me at all. She is way too loud...always, and not body shaming but she is really... ill-built.

I only know her because a homeboy of mine from years ago, hooked up with her friend, and she *thought* she was gonna hook up with me. I wouldn't fuck her with my enemy's dick.

I barely have conversations with her whenever I see her. I get the hell outta dodge every time. And this time will be no different.

Zariah clears her throat, causing me to look her way, "So we using *full* government names, Bleu? You might wanna handle this. And expeditiously." She nods toward the entrance, sitting back in her seat, arms crossed, raising her eyebrows, waiting to see how I handle it as she not so subtly suggests.

"Heyyyy, Boo!" Anise staggers to a stop in front of me.

"Anise? Why are you always *so* loud?" I ask, my voice dripping in disgust.

"JP, you so funny, boy." She lightly taps my chest and batting those caterpillar lashes.

"Mmph... she's calling *all* the names," Zariah mutters and rolling her eyes.

"Baby..." Redd warns.

Anise leans in for a hug that I sidestep with the quickness. Even if Mila wasn't staring daggers into me, I never let her touch me, the fuck!

"What are you doing, Anise? You know we not like that."

"Awww, JPeeeee! We always had a spark." She slurs, trips—right into Redd's lap.

Zariah's eyes narrow.

Redd freezes, hands instantly shoot up, hovering midair like he's being arrested. Anise wiggles. "I see someone's happy to see me."

"Bitch!"

"Anise!"

"Baby!"

Whyte is off to the side, sitting at the next table cackling. Zariah hops up from her seat, quick as fuck, and slings Anise's drunken body off Redd's lap.

Redd's shocked facial expression never changes.

Anise stumbles over her feet landing into my chest.

I step back and throw my hands outward like *whoa*, as she steadies herself.

This shit is like the world's worst sitcom happening in real time.

I see Whyte pull out his phone. "Nah, Jay. Stay jussst liiiike that!" He takes a picture, nodding toward a very pissed off Mila, heading in our direction.

"Fuck me running..." I mutter.

"I will!" Anise hollers.

"Anise! Shut. The fuck. Up!"

It's as if God really hates me because right now, all my eyes see is an angry, thick, lil' light brown skin lady, with wild, reddish-brown hair, and beautiful caramel brown eyes, blazing, walking quickly toward me. Slanting said eyes as she watches Anise clinging to me.

Damn! She looks good. Mila storms in wearing a slinky black silk slip dress that clings in all the right places, a sheer cream duster, low-top black Chucks on her feet, a dainty diamond anklet that catches the light with each step she takes, and large, gold hoops framing her face. Her hair in its natural curly state looking like a ring of fire dancing about as she moves. Even pissed and hungover, she looks like a walking dare: Say something slick, and watch what happens.

"Please leave, Anise." I push her off, but it's too late, Mila's already here.

"But JP..." she whines, making a sloppy attempt to hang onto me.

Mila slides in between us, pinches Anise's hand between her thumb and index finger like her hand is diseased, removing it from my person and dropping it midair, while me and the crew lose it. Zariah hollers, Redd chokes on his drink, Whyte doubles over. And me? Watching my woman handle business? Got my dick hard. God help me, I love this woman. And Anise, she's clueless as ever.

Looking down into the face of *the love of my life*, I can tell she's hungover but she's too pissy right now to let it show.

"Good morning, my love," I say, grinning.

"Absolutely not. The fuck is this?" Mila points between me and Anise. My ring glitters under the light, beautiful and blinding.

"Sweet—"

"No thank you. And what the fuck is this?!" She shoves her ring finger in my face, eyes daring me to answer.

Shit. Anise isn't the problem anymore.

# Chapter 3
# Mila

***S****ame Morning, An hour ago...*

I finally steady myself enough to wash up, throw on clothes, and follow the note Bleu left me down to the hotel restaurant. My head is pounding, my body feels like it's carrying bricks. I should know better. Lupus doesn't let me get away with shit for free. Fun always comes with guilt and flare-ups, but dammit, it was so worth it.

The elevator ride has me dizzy as hell. It does nothing for my hungover state, so I tilt my head toward the security camera, like I'm leaving breadcrumbs in case something happens. Trauma response, I guess. I'm always mapping exits, avoiding sitting with my back to doors. Sometimes I swear I was in witness protection in another life.

"This is the longest elevator ride in history, jeez!" I whisper aloud to myself. Finally, what seems like at least 10 minutes, but was probably only maybe 1 or 2 in reality, the elevator doors open into the corridor and to my left is the entrance into the hotel restaurant.

By the time I step into the Venetian's restaurant, I'm struck by how opulent this place is — marble, columns, chandeliers. I design spaces like this in my dreams. I know Bleu gets tired of me rambling about design, but I can't help it. Plus, that's part of the job he campaigned for and got, so....

And then I see him.

Talking to her. Who is this bitch?

She's too close, too familiar. And the cause of all this havoc: Zariah's scolding Redd, Whyte doubles over laughing. Bleu looks... trapped.

I walk in between the two of them, removing this trick off my man. My husband. Or at least I think he's my husband.

I take my left hand, diamonds from my ring glittering brightly, and with my index finger and thumb, I remove her hand off Bleu's chest and drop it as if it were trash. He stands back a bit, looking down at me with those beautiful, blue hooded eyes and that shit eating grin on his face.

"Good morning, my love," he says, grinning.

"Absolutely not. The fuck is this?" I point between him and this annoying ass chick.

"Sweet-"

"No thank you. And what the fuck is this?!" I shove my ring finger in his face, eyes daring him to answer.

Lord knows I didn't want to discuss my business in front of whoever this woman is, but he provokes and evokes me to no end.

This fool gently takes my hand and kisses the back of it, the ring, and the palm of my hand. He then places it on his heart, stepping as close to me as humanly possible.

"Eh hmm." Sounds from behind me. Knowing how I feel about watching my back, Bleu slowly sways and turns us to where ol' girl is on the side of us, as opposed to behind me, where I can't see her.

"Act like you know, JP!" Cara screams from a nearby table she's leaning on, laughing her butt off. Where'd she come from? I didn't see her when I walked in.

Ignoring whoever this girl is, I got bigger fish to fry. I can guarantee you, JaCaryous does NOT want to fuck around and find out.

"Try again, sir. Why do I have this exquisite ring on my ring finger, Mr. Patrick? I can remember bits and pieces of yesterday, only to wake up this morning to what looks like an engagement ring on my hand."

"Wedding ring."

"What?! So, WE..." I motion between him and me, "are truly married?"

"Sweet, you wound me yet again." He grabs his chest as if it aches. "You've been Mrs. Patrick since before we officially met. So, I don't know what you want me to say."

"JaCaryous! Quit playing with me!"

"Ummm, helloooo!" the unknown woman attempts to interrupt again. Who *is* this trick?

Just as I turn to resolve who the hell she is, Zariah is physically redirecting her like she does her patients.

"Nooooo. No. No. No. Let's give this lovely couple some space. You've done enough for one day. Go get some coffee... and a bath, sober up. Be safe and Godspeed," Zariah firmly grabs her shoulders and moves with her, pushing her toward the exit.

"Man, yo' girls know when to come in clutch! I swear!" Bleu yells.

"JaCaryous, please! Did we get married last night for real?" Searching his face for any clue, my eyes beg him to answer me.

"Aww shawty, you know I fuck wit' you the long way." Grinning at me like a fool, I glare at him.

"Bleu, what does that even mean?!" I throw my hands in the air exasperated.

"ARE WE MARRIED?!"

"Mi, what's understood don't need to be explained."

"Oh, my Godddddd!" I scream in frustration, turn, and walk away.

"Aye, Mi!" he yells out behind me.

I stop walking and turn to face him. Finally, he's going to answer me.

"I sholl hate to see you –"

"Don't even, Bleu!" I turn back towards the exit and storm away, hearing those stupid asses cackling from the table behind me. I don't have time for this foolishness and clearly nothing is getting resolved now. I am going back to bed. My head is killing me!

*** 

A few hours later, I wake up from a very much needed nap but no Bleu, again. That's not like him, I wonder where he is? Even though my headache has subsided, the body aches are beginning to set in. I know I've done more than the absolute most this past week and my body is about to remind me who is in charge, seeking total world domination on me while trying to repair itself.

Lying here, willing myself to move, I take in how quiet the space is without Bleu. And I don't know how to feel about it. It's too quiet. I've gotten used to him *always* being around, hovering.

Where is he? Did I do too much earlier? It's always the quiet that exacerbates these doubts and insecurities. I don't think I did too much. Right? The least he could do is give me a straight answer to if we are legally married or not. What's most shocking to me right now is that I'm quite comfortable rolling with Bleu, married or not. And if I'm being honest with myself, I kinda hope we *are* married.

I don't know who I am right now. Last week's Mila would have been posted up outside the county clerk's office on Sunday waiting until they opened Monday. I'm not this person. Everything has to be done in decency and in order. I hate surprises. Ok, that's not true. I actually love surprises but only the good kind. I miss that part of me that can trust that everything will be ok, without a plan. Only having myself to depend on for so long doesn't leave much room in my life for spontaneity. This. This...feels...nice.

I smile softly at the thought. Missing Beu even more. Bleu blew into my life like this soft but very intentional breeze, mixed with the right amounts of warmth and coolness. He's just so all consuming. He told me repeatedly he was coming for me all gas, no brakes. He told me at the café, he told me in the nail shop, he told me at the party, Redd & Zariah's house, the waterfront. He *told* me. I saw his lips moving. I watched his actions. But I had no clue he meant every word he said. But what else do I expect from this man? My man. He caters to me, nurtures me, dare I say... loves me. My days have been nothing less than boring since I've laid eyes on him... this time.

I struggle, hard, with the fact that all of this has happened within the span of a week. We have always been aware the other existed and even seen each other in passing before. But is it realistic to *know* this is your person so quickly? I need to discuss this with Nicole. Maybe I don't. The thought of me upsetting him or not being with him makes me physically ill. My therapist doesn't have to reframe any of this for me. My logic is tussling with my emotions heavy. That's the real issue. My emotions aren't used to being acknowledged, mostly used in important decision making.

"Get over yourself, Mi. You loved that man almost instantaneously. You would have never done half the things you have with him if you didn't. You wouldn't feel the way you do. You wouldn't feel like your life is over if you were not actually married to him," I say to myself.

"Ugh, dramatic much." I roll my eyes, chuckling.

My phone lights up with a text.

> **Cara**: Bitch, meet me at the Juliet Cocktail Bar in an hour. Don't make me come get you.

Chuckling, I don't bother to respond. I check my call and text log, no Bleu. Hmm. That's not like him. I call him, only to be met with the voicemail. My stomach drops. He never not answers for me. I don't leave a message. I lay back on the pillow, playing through all the intrusive thoughts swirling through my mind.

A few minutes pass, needing the distraction, I drag myself out of the bed, stretching, and flop back down. My body screams, stay in bed. My mind says, it's Vegas, Baby! And my heart? My heart is just... tired. And a little frightened. I miss Bleu.

I pull on a comfy, cute two-piece from TikTok shop. I add a couple of gold pieces and head out to meet Cara. Walking slowly, I take in the scenery as I move into the Grand Colonnade, sunlight spilling through tall windows, bouncing off marble floors so polished they look wet. Tourists drag rolling suitcases, couples pause to take selfies under the gilded arches, and everywhere I look, there's more artistic detail—ornate moldings, frescoed ceilings, carved columns that make me itch to sketch them later.

My goodness, the thick, lush carpets swallow my footsteps as I follow the walkway across the casino floor. Everything glitters. I keep telling myself to savor this, take it all in. My designer brain goes into overdrive just as my body reminds me I've overdone it. Stupid Lupus!

"Oh wow," I whisper in awe of the décor when a rush of vertigo hits hard and fast, tilting the room like the *tilt a world* carnival ride. Not wanting to draw attention to myself I press closer to the wall for support. There's a seating area ahead, thank God. I'll just sit for a second to gather myself.

This bench cushion is quite divine thick, soft, upholstered in a fabric that feels like clouds. I sink down, running my hand across the seam, admiring the workmanship.

"Focus, crazy," I mutter, shaking my head. "You drooling over a cushion when you could hit the floor any second. You've been doing way too much this week. Getcho' mind right." I chastise myself.

After about a minute, the spinning eases. I push myself up slow and continue down Restaurant Row. The aroma of truffle oil, roasted garlic, and espresso floats through the air as I pass by glossy eateries, each one fascinating, in its own right.

Finally, after what seems like the longest walk in history, the *Juliet Cocktail Room* comes into view dimly lit, sultry, with velvet curtains pulled back to reveal a jewel-box of a space. I spot Cara immediately, lounging in an open booth like she owns the joint.

As I slide into the booth across from Cara, the waitress is setting down her drink, and I order a virgin Piña Colada.

"What's the occasion?" I ask.

"Don't know. But aren't congratulations in order?" She is looking at me curiously.

"Congratulations for who? I don't have anything to celebrate."

Cara smirks. "So y'all didn't get married last night?"

Exhaling loudly, "I don't know, that's the damn problem! I woke up with this five-carat aquamarine diamond twisty platinum wedding set..." I wiggle my finger.

Her eyes widen. "Wait. You woke up with a wedding ring...this ring? And no memory of the wedding?"

"Mmhhmm. And to add insult to injury, Bleu won't confirm or deny said marriage."

"What did he say?"

"You were there this morning at the restaurant when he was spewing all that dumb shit, 'Mi, what's understood don't need to be explained. *Aww Sweet, you wound me... You've **been** Mrs. Patrick... ...What you want me to say?*" I'm doing my best Bleu impersonation.

"Nigga, say yes, we are legally married or no, we are not, damn!"

Witnessing my frustration but knowing I am not lying about her friend, JaCaryous, Cara doubles over crying with laughter.

"And yet," she says when she catches her breath, "you're sitting here calm, not knowing your legal last name."

"Whatchu mean?"

Cara side-eyes me. "Ma'am, BB, Before Bleu your anxiety wouldn't have let this slide, you would've had a panic attack not knowing your last name. But look at you now, sitting pretty with a mystery marriage like it's a spa day."

I roll my eyes, but she's right. With Bleu, it's different. I can breathe. I trust him.

She studies me, then grins. "Bitch, you love him."

"Cah-raaaahhhh, I love hiiiiimmm," I tell her in my whiny teenager voice.

"I dooo."

"You dooo."

"See! You're sitting here with this faraway look on your face, eyes all glossed over like everything is sweet. No pun intended. I know I tease but this is a real good look on you, Mi. I'm happy for you."

"I'm scared though."

"Of?"

"Did we move to soon? Will this work? Is he sane? Can he handle me?"

"Listen, Mi. It's ok to ask those questions and more. Look at it like this, whether you're married today or two years from now, those questions will still run through your mind. You and Bleu have the love and capacity to dedicate yourselves to the marriage and one another to make it work."

"Yeah?"

"Yeah..." she agrees softly. "Life is filled with surprises, ups, and downs. Who better to experience it with than a man who loves you completely?"

"Yeah!" I grin enthusiastically. Lifting my glass, "To me and my assumed marriage."

Clinking her glass with mine, "To you and your blessed marriage! Salud!"

# Chapter 4

# Redd

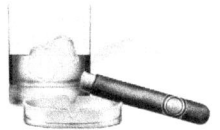

*V*egas, Still Same Day

"Come here, ma." I pat the seat next to me, gesturing for Zariah to sit next to me.

"Whassup, my love?"

"Man, shit was crazy last night."

"Shits been crazy. Mi and Bleu, Cara and Whyte. This whole week has been like a movie."

"Yeah, this Cara and Whyte situation. What is that about? They be actin' like the can't stand to breathe the same air but was giving off *come fuck me* vibes."

Waving her hand, "Who knows for real? I'm just sitting back and observing. I got my own shit to contend with, much less anyone else's." Of course I know she knows what's going on with Cara and Whyte, but she'll say, "It's not my story to tell." My wife is the true keeper of secrets. She won't betray her girls' privacy.

"What kind of shit you got to contend with that your man can't handle for you?" Pressing my hand to her flat belly.

"You know I gotchu, boo."

"Yeah..."

She pauses, "I don't know. Baby, I feel happy, but I'm also terrified. This is supposed to one of the happiest times of our lives, right? We're supposed to be ecstatic. And I mean, I am excited and happy but I'm also really nervous." I feel like her truth gut punches me. Here I am, thinking we are on the same page and we're not? I didn't know she was having these kinds of concerns. I pull her close, not trusting my facial expression. I thought she was just as excited as me. I pull us back on the sofa, hug her close to me, giving us both time to collect ourselves.

"Listen Zi, I'm on whatchu on. If you think this may not be good timing then... you know...we can..."

"Wait, wait! I'm not saying definitively that I don't want to be pregnant and have your little one. I was just sharing my thoughts."

"Whew, ok! I thought you was trying to get rid of Deuce before lil' man even had a chance."

She snatches away from me, bucking her eyes, "Fuck Redd! Pressure much?! See, this is why I didn't even want to have this stupid ass conversation! How am I supposed to process this without feeling guilty about my feelings?"

"Baby, baby, baby, hold on!" I rear back in shock.

"I'm just excited is all, but you know I am *always* gonna ride with you. I can't say I fully understand exactly how you're feeling, BUT... I trust your judgment. If I'm being honest, the timing is a little off but hell, I was just gonna rock with it. I know there's nothing that I, we, can't do without each other. We got family here that's hella supportive, so there's that. Come here." I stand her up and wipe the tears from her face. I wrap her tight in my arms until I feel her physically relax against my body.

"Thank you." She murmurs in my chest. "I'm sorry. You always calm my crazy. I love you so much, Redd."

"I know, baby. I love you so much more. And you know they always say the most brilliant mental health professionals are the batshit crazy ones." Laughing, I dodge her tiny hits to my chest and arms.

"There's my girl. Come on, Belle. Let me treat my favorite girl to something good. You up for a Vegas adventure?"

She blushes at me calling her nickname I gave her when we were kids.

"As if you have to ask. You haven't called me Belle in forever. I thought you might have forgotten…"

"Never that. Shiiit, you'll always be my Belle. You're my Beauty and I'm your Beast, no cap." I love feeling her shiver when I nip the spot where her neck and shoulder meet.

"RJ, stop." She whines but doesn't stop me.

I continue nipping across her shoulders and the back of her neck. "That's what you want, Belle? You want me to stop? Hmm?" I place my hand beneath her shirt and under her bra while sucking her neck. Tweaking her nipples until they stand firm. Her breathing becomes more audible and quickens in pace. I don't even think she notices I'm walking her into the bedroom. "I can't hear you, Belle."

"I, I, mmmm… Redd!"

"Yeah, baby, you, you, what? *Dis à papa que tu le veux. (Tell daddy you want it.)*"

"I remember what that means, nasty. Uhn, Redd!"

"Then tell Daddy you want it. Stop bullshittin', Zariah."

"You know I want it, baby, you fuck me so good. Ahhh, make me feel that shit."

"I gotchu." Pushing my shorts further down and pulling the front of my shirt over my head. Bending her over the bed, I bend my knees and a dip, pushing my dick into her wet, tight tunnel. I start power driving her lil' ass. The only sounds in the room are our moans, grunts, and my balls slapping her ass repeatedly. I didn't even fully undress her before diving into that pussy.

"This shit so wet and tight. Gat damn pregnant pussy...my gawd tahday!"

"Tell me what you need, Belle. Don't get quiet on me now." I keep dipping in her shit, hitting her spot over and over with every stroke.

"I...ca- can't!"

"I feel you tightening up on me, whatchu waiting on? Let that shit go, Belle!"

"Baaa- ooo... I feel that shit in my- uhn, ahhh... Cum with me baby, wet me up!"

"Shiiit, say less. You want this muhfuckin' nut, here it is!"

"Anhh, Redddddd!"

"Unnnhhhhh!" I double over, holding her back to my chest tight, trying to catch my breath as we both cum together. Woo, shit! I swear the bones in my toes are cracking the fuck open.

Slapping her right ass cheek, "If you wasn't already pregnant, you would be now, no doubt. Hold still so I can lay you down and clean you."

I completely remove my shorts and head into the bathroom to get a warm, soapy towel to clean my girl. She's knocked out by the time I return, so I remove her clothes and gently clean her. Covering her up, I throw my shorts back on, pull the door up, and go into the living room.

Pulling the blunt from behind my ear, I fire that bitch up and lay my head back on the couch. I try to be supportive but real talk, if Zi don't want my baby, this could potentially be the beginning of the end of our marriage. *Wait! What the fuck am I saying?* Where did that thought even come from? I love my wife. I'm *in love* with my wife. I've loved this girl since as far back as I can remember. There's never not been Zariah in my life. Ever. I guess I gotta get ready for whatever she may decide. I sure hope she chooses right.

Phone vibrating on the table, it's this nigga, Whyte. "Whaddup, nigga?"

"Fuck wrong with you? You good, yeah?"

"Yeah, I'm just chilling in the room. Zi is napping. I just lit one. Whassup? Where y'all at?"

"Ain't no y'all. You know Bleu is all up Mila's ass. And Cara ain't got shit for me...again. I was seeing if you could get out, maybe smoke something, drink something, eat something. Ion know."

"I gotchu. Ion wanna leave Zi. She's in a weird headspace right now."

"Word? Nigga, what you do?""Me? I haven't done a thing. She's weirding out about the baby."

"Ah, ok. Well, I'll leave you to it. I know that's a heavy topic. And I don't want to intrude."

"I told you she sleep, nigga. Come through. We can order something to eat. I got plenty to smoke and you brang the drank."

"Bet, I'm heading that way."

"Cool." I disconnect the call, jump in the shower real quick before Whyte gets here.

A few minutes later this fool is beat boxing on the door. Snatching the door open, I glare at his ass.

"Nigga, you can't knock like a normal nigga? I told you Zi is sleep."

"Shiiiitt, if she still sleep like she did when we were kids, you could drop a bomb on her ass and she still would not wake up."

Laughing, I dap his ass up, "Get off my wife, nigga. Find you something else safe to play with."

"Ol' sensitive ass nigga." He laughs, shoving my shoulder.

I grab a couple of these heavy ass crystal glasses and pour us up. Whyte ordered us some wings and sliders and shit, and I pass him a newly rolled blunt. We're both quiet and in deep thought passing the blunt while sipping and listening to the water feature in the suite. Whyte breaks the silence.

"Aight, nigga. What's got you in yo' head? You sound like a wounded seal when I called."

"Bruh, how does a...? You know what, never mind." Exhaling loudly, "I told you Zariah is conflicted about the pregnancy. You know ever since we were kids, it's been me and Zi. At least in my mind, I figured we would get married, have a few kids, and shit would be gravy. I never thought she would have second thoughts about havin' a nigga's baby."

"I'm trying to be supportive and shit. Ultimately, I'm on what she on type shit but I can't lie, a nigga's chest tight, thinking my wife might not want my kid."

"Damn, nigga. She know any of this?"

"I mean, I tried to express that shit and I think she heard me but Ion know 'cause she switched up on a nigga so fast."

"Switch up, whatchu mean?" "Pass me that blunt. Her moods, nigga. Like I get seven seconds of honest transparency from her, then when I respond, I get blessed with another 30 seconds of crazy. If that's what a nigga gonna have to experience, shit!"

"Whatchu gone do, LB?"

"Support my wife, keep my thoughts and emotions to myself, and hope for the best."

"I'm no relationship expert. Or no counselor or no shit but Ion think that's how that's 'spose to go. Ain't y'all 'spose to be open and honest and shit?"

"Yeah. But look where it gets me.""Where, nigga? Sitting on the sofa, choppin' it up witcho day one?" This nigga smirks at me, passing the blunt.

"Fuck outta here." Toking and passing it back to Whyte, I lean my head back on the couch, closing my eyes. Unaware that Zariah hears the entire conversation.

Whyte leaves close to two hours later and I return to the bedroom to check on Zariah. Her back is facing the door. She looks like she's still sleeping. I grab some clean underwear and go to take a full shower. The quick one from earlier wasn't enough. Plus, I want to get the smoke and alcohol smell off me. I finish in the shower and moisturize my body. I spend some time on my face and beard, then brush my teeth and tongue before swishing this minty ass mouthwash. After completing my hygiene regimen, I feel a bit more relaxed.

I gather my things, open the door to walk out of the bathroom and back into the bedroom, and Zariah is standing there.

"Zi! Why you just standing there creepin' on a nigga?"

She laughs, "Actually, I wasn't. I was coming into the bathroom just as you opened the door. Why you so jumpy? Guilty of something, RJ?"

"What? Nah. What would I be guilty off? You know a nigga's every move, Zi." I'm looking everywhere but directly at her. She clocks it and knows when I'm hiding something.

"Baby, come sit with me."

She gently grabs my hands and pulls me in the direction of the two chairs opposite the bed.

"Whassup, Zi?"

"Listen. I was awake and could hear you and Whyte talking earlier."

I drop my head, waiting for the backlash and drama.

"Zariah..."

"No, baby, wait. I want to apologize to you for making you feel like you can't be real with me. Hormones and bullshit aside, we're in this together. It's just you and me."

"And the baby."

"Yes, and the baby. I want to create a safe space for you to communicate your true feelings with me at any and all times."

"Babe, you don't have to therapize me. I'm not one of your patients."

"I know that, Redd, and I'm not trying to treat you like one. But I also need you to normalize..."

I raise my eyebrow to prove my point.

"To get in the habit of being comfortable with talking to me about any and everything. We been in this too long for us not to. And for the record, sometimes I may use what *you* might call "therapy words" but that doesn't mean I am trying to be your therapist. The roles that I want to have in your life, is that of your wife, your friend, your confidante, your peace, your slut..."

"Awww shit, now we talking!"

I pull her out of her chair and into my lap.

"And what else, baby? What other roles you wanna have in my life, Zi?" I lift her shirt, allowing my hands to take up residence all over her body.

"What roles you need me to have, RJ?" she asks seductively, while placing soft kisses on my lips.

"I mean, you pretty much covered them all. But let's revisit your role as my slut. Tell me, Dr. Jackson, what does that look like?"

Placing the tip of her index finger between her teeth, "Well, Daddy, it looks like you having your way with me. However. You. Like."

"Consensually of course," she adds.

"Mmmhmm, tell me more."

Pressing her mouth to mine, licking the outer rim of my tongue, she whispers several different ways that she knows I would love to slut her out, in grave detail. Before she could blink good, I impale her on this hard ass dick, making her make good on her suggestions.

# Chapter 5

# BLEU

**V**egas, Same day, *Later that evening....*

We finish dinner in the private dining room I reserved. Looking around, no better time than the present, I stand with my glass in my hand surveying everyone at the dinner table. I glance down at Mila and she is *not* fuckin' wit' a nigga...at all. She will after this though. Her mood has been off ever since I got back in the room earlier.

*"Oh, so you finally decide to come back. Where've you been all day, Bleu, I called you."*

*"I know, Sweet. I'm sorry. I've been moving all day."* *Pressing a quick peck on her forehead, I walk past her to get*

*my outfit together for tonight. I can feel her eyes lasering into my back.*

*"Okaayy....that's it?"*

*I turn to look at her. "Yeah, I mean... I don't want us to be late to dinner, Sweet." I turn my back to her again, this time smirking. She wants to beat my ass right now, but if we can just make it to dinner, it'll all be worth it.*

*"What are you wearing tonight, my love?"*

*She breezes past me, slamming the bathroom door in response to my question.*

I lightly tap my glass with my fork. "Alright, alright. I want to thank everyone for all the love and support over the past week. I pray everyone had a great time. I especially want to thank my wife, Mila Nicole Patrick, for not only trusting me with her heart in such a short period of time but *legally* trusting me with her life and making me the happiest and most blessed man alive."

She whips her head in my direction, glossy eyes shining, standing, and crashing into my arms. Redd, Cara, Whyte, and Zariah all cheer us on and congratulate us.

"Mi, I know you was mad at a nigga earlier, but I was doing all of this for you. And I know this morning I wouldn't confirm nor deny if we had legally gotten married." Keeping my eyes trained on hers, I sit my glass down and reach into my pocket to retrieve the matching band to her ring. She gasps lightly.

"Sweet, you may have given me the silent treatment today and was frustrated with me, but you also showed me that you trust me. And I know for a fact you love a nigga." I smirk.

She laughs through her tears. Everyone else chuckles.

"I know we got married on what appeared to be a whim. And you don't remember it, but I promise you this was premeditated and put in the works the moment you agreed to come to Vegas. Mi. Baby. I could never cheat you out of a precious moment like this."

I bend on one knee in front of her. Her hands fly to her face, covering her mouth as tears fall from her eyes.

"I have loved you from the very first moment I saw you. I was determined then to make you, well *legally* make you, Mrs. JaCaryous K. Patrick. Mila Nicole Sutton – Patrick, will you do me the honor of continuing to be my lawfully wedded wife?" I ask her as I slide the wedding ring off, put the matching band on, and return the ring to its rightful place. Kissing the ring on her finger, I wait for her answer.

Crying, she shakes her head vigorously.

"Use your words, Sweet. I need to hear you love me."

"Yes! Yes! It will be *my* honor to remain Mrs. Mila Nicole Patrick."

As soon as I heard the first *yes*, I jump up, pulling her to me, crushing our lips together. Our kiss is a vow of forever. When we finally break apart, I lift her little ass to me so she's eye level, "I told you that you were Mrs. Patrick." I place a wet sloppy kiss on her lips, and she throws her head back laughing.

Our friends surround us, hugging and celebrating us.

"Man, this is truly a holiday celebration we will never forget," Redd shouts.

Whyte grabs and raises his glass, "A toast to two of the most deserving people I know. Now that love has found you, may it keep you, hold you, and grow you. Salud!"

# Act 2

# Chapter 6

# Weston William Whyte

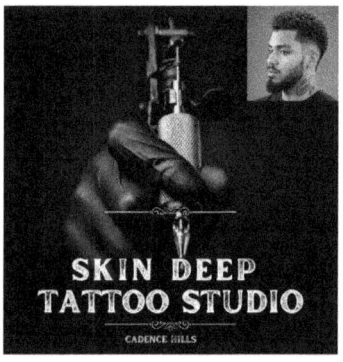

**J**uly 6<sup>th</sup>

### Back to Cadence, Back to Reality

Whew! A nigga is ti-erred. Usually, this holiday week every year is on go but *this year...* leave it to that nigga Bleu to up the game. As the girls call it, a week of shenanigans, Vegas, and a marriage. I couldn't be happier for my two best friends coming together and making that shit official. When that nigga said no brakes, all gas, he wasn't bullshittin'. I kinda admire my LB's tenacity.

In hindsight, I have to admit I was skeptical as fuck about him going after Mi. Me and Bleu go way back. We're line brothers and I consider him one of my best friends.

His track record wasn't bad per se but from the first day I met Mila on campus, I've had this need to protect her like one of my sisters. I don't know, she just had, well, still has, this quiet vulnerability about her. Her exterior appears unbothered, almost closed off. But the reality is she's used to being alone and having to weather life's storms that aren't easy for anyone, much less someone that has no one.

Not that I pity her, never that. I admire her and I just want to be a soft place for her to land if and when she needs it. She deserves it. I guess now I can somewhat pass the torch.

"What's got you in your head?" she asks, breaking me out of my reverie.

"Just thinking about this week's events. Shit happened so fast, it's almost surreal. Whatchu think about ya' girl getting married? Give you the warm and fuzzies?" I tease, pulling Cara into my arms. Our history is so tumultuous. Me wanting her and her wanting any and everything but a relationship. I know she could care less about marriage.

She stiffens just a bit but not before schooling her features, showing no emotions, only as Miss Love does, "Shit, if they like it, I love it. Couldn't be me though."

I sit up, leaning back against my headboard, bracing myself for this bullshit rhetoric she spews. I pretty much know it by heart.

"Yeah, yeah, we know. You on yo' grown woman shit. Before you know it, you gonna look up alone one day on yo' *old* woman shit."

She looks back at me and if looks could kill…. I press my luck and continue.

"It's cool though. I fucks wit' it until I don't." I place a wet, noisy kiss on her forehead, knowing she hates that shit. I'm tired of her treating me like straight street booty. Using a nigga for his dick and denying all the feelings that we both know are there.

So, this time, I beat her to the punch, "Aye, but I got some shit to take care of, so you're more than welcome to stay if you want. Lock up when you leave." I roll her gently off me to her side and get up to head to the shower, but not before slapping her on her ass and winking at her. Cara's shock is an understatement. She's livid.

Check. Muthafuckin' Mate.

# Chapter 7

# Cara Love

"Uggh! I swear. To. Gawd! I hate that nigga!" I'm so mad I can't see straight, stomping to my car, trying to get the fuck away from him. After slamming the door and starting my car, the music fills my space and of course my life plays out like this fucking song. I hate him, Trey Songz's, and Summer Walker's asses right now.

Nobody told her to sing my emotions to me, "Argh!" I am literally screaming and beating the steering wheel right now. I wish I didn't care for Whyte like I do. I wish the fear that dictates my hearts actions was non-existent.

*Why are you so hard to leave?Why are you so hard to believe?Can't you make it easy for me?*

"Of course, the fuck not, he can't. He won't. He knows. And he knows I know that he knows."

*I complicate in my brainSwear to God you make me go insaneYou love me then you make me feel a way...*

Fuck! Fuck! Fuck! I refuse to cry! Too late... the tears are scorching the interior of my eye sockets and I'm not sure that I can stop them from falling. "What is wrong with me?"

*...You get on my last damn nervesThen I say that I'm done...*

"Quit playing dumb bitch, you know what it is." As if she hadn't just confirmed my thoughts...

*...So if this isn't love*

Wiping my eyes, I head to my spot. That one line stays on repeat in my head:

*...So if this isn't love*

*** 

For the last week I've been "processing" as Zi would say and I can finally own my feelings AND say them out loud. I love him. I'm *in love* with Whyte. He knows it. Hell, everyone knows it. Thinking back to the conversation with Mila and Zariah a few days ago, I had invited them over to talk about my feelings because I felt like I was going crazy.

*"Hey, Sorors." I invited them in.*

*They removed their shoes, looking at each other and questioning me simultaneously, "Sorors?"*

*"Bitch, is this a hostage situation? You know that's not the code word!" Mila whisper-yelled.*

*"Absolutely not. Why are you like this?" I asked her.*

*"Me?" She pointed to herself.*

"*Since when do we greet each other saying some, '**Hey, Sorors?**'*"

*I rolled my eyes and headed to the balcony. "Girl, c'mon."*

*Following me out there, Zariah complimented me on the spread of appetizers and drinks once saw*

*Zi sat and said, "Alright, what is it?" Mila sat quietly, me to speak.*

*"So... I know we don't keep things from each other. I needed time, a lot of time,*

*to figure this thing out and process it, I guess. For about a year now, Whyte and I have been hanging out, mmm... more like hooking up. It started with friendly convos and you know he's such a flirt. I'd come home and we'd hang out sometimes, which isn't abnormal. That's what we all do.*

*I paused to take a sip of my drink. Why am I so uncomfortable talking about this? These are*

*"So yeah. I... you know with my work travel, I can be gone for weeks, months even, at a*

*time. And you know I got needs. They don't stop because of my work schedule. So we hooked up once and swore it was a mistake. We agreed not to do it again. Obviously, that didn't work, it's a year later and here I still am."*

*Looking at them, I ask, "Y'all ain't got nothing to say?" They both shook their heads **no**, so I continue.*

*"Bet, so yeah, I don't know what to do about... about how I'm feeling about this whole situation."*

*Mila got the biggest grin on her face and started softly clapping. She looked like she was about to jump out of her seat.*

*"Whaaaat, MiMi? What do you have to say?"*

*Still grinning, "Nothing. Please continue."*

*"Look, we fucked around when I was in town sometimes and then he started "servicing" ,,,got, tried, soBut after*

*"Your ego." Mila interjected.*

*I continued speaking, ignoring her comment.* "He told me that he would be cordial so we would not d.

"Mila, to your ego comment, I texted an apology to him that he ignored. And he's been

**Silence.** *Ok, I'll keep going.*

"My dilemma is, I'm completely lost on if I want a relationship. If I do, what does that look "

"My dad has been a single dad forever. And my brothers are no help. They fuck for sport. I could go back to using my escorts, these niggas fuck for work. They provide all the hot sex with none of the extra shit that I either don't know how to deal with or want to deal with."

*I sit back in my seat and loudly exhale.* "That shit is crazy! I've avoided emotions and shit "

**Fuckin' Whyte! Well, fuckin' Whyte is how I got here.** *I laugh to myself. The irony.*

"Can you tricks say something?"

*Mila asked,* "What do you want us to say? Forever, you've had this "I don't shit where I eat …

"And I knew y'all had been together. I didn't know details or how long." *Zariah shrugged her ed*

*Taking another deep breath, I began again,* "Mila. What did you mean when you said **my**

"Cara, we've been cool way too long for you to think I don't know you better than you know ,,

"You're hurt. And when you hurt you become **very mean**. Your words **cut**, cuz chile, yo'

"That's funny. One thing Whyte said before he left was that my mouth was reckless. I

*Zariah grabbed my hand into hers.* "What do you need from us? Do you just need to vent and

*I gently pulled my hand from hers, hugging myself. If I could roll into a tight ball and shut the world out I would. Zariah knew what I was doing when I removed my hand from hers. Mila came, sat on the opposite side of me and*

*pulled me into a hug. I didn't reciprocate but I was sure glad
she wouldn't let me go. I needed this.*

*After a few minutes of us all sitting quietly, Mila checked
with me, "So whatchu gone do,*

*I lifted my head from her shoulder, trying to make the
words in my head and heart make sense.*

*"Aight Joe, check this out." Mila said as she moved back to
her seat.*

*"Aww shit, she finna Chi-town me. Anytime she begins a
sentence with "Aight Joe, check*

*"Fah real, CiCi. You like this dude. If you didn't, you
wouldn't be sending SOS texts to us to come over and have
this very conversation. And you wouldn't be treating poor
Whyte like he did something wrong by catching feelings for
you. And I bet you everything in your bank account that that
little funky ass "apology"..." she said using air quotes, "that
you claim to have "texted"... " again with air quotes, "Whyte
was some dumb shit like, "my bad"—"*

*Interrupting her, I corrected, "I texted him, "forgive me"
and then added the color hearts*

*"Bitch, Ima beatcho ass for Whyte," she said matter of
factly.*

*"I knoooww," I groaned.*

*"Cara, we, you, are too grown and too accomplished to
insult that man and yourself by*

*"Period," Zariah added.*

*"Cara, first order of business is to sort out your feelings.
And if you're afraid, it's ok. This is new and it's a huge
step for you. And possibly new for him, too. Once you have
come to grips with the fact that you would like to entertain a
monogamous, committed, intimate, adult relationship with
Weston William Whyte, then call him, meet with him in
person, and give that man the apology he deserves. Tell him
how you feel about him. Let him dick you down with that*

*demon he has between his legs and then all will be right in the world.*

And *THAT* is my biggest problem. Well, one of them, that demon between his legs and my past. My past and my trauma won't let me act on my emotions and desires. I'm so afraid of not being enough. And getting hurt. That I'll do almost anything to avoid being vulnerable. I never learned how to be soft and it doesn't come easy to a girl who grew up in a house filled with males and no positive or female roles models. I know now that my brothers and my dad had fucked me up, watching how they treated females and the lessons of what not to let a nigga do. And while I'm happy for Mila and Zariah, that's their lot in life. Love is not in the cards for me. The only love I feel is the love of money. That's the one consistent in my life that won't hurt me. I'm set for life on that front.

The soft purr of my cell phone interrupts my thoughts, the dash lights up, causing a bright smile to appear on my face. I hit the phone icon on my steering wheel.

"Kash baby, you ready to line my pockets?"

"Cara, you ready to bring that sexy ass back to Europe?"

Without taking a beat to think about his question, "How soon are we talking, I just got back from Vegas?"

"I've got a G7 idling. I'm just waiting for you, love. Your chariot awaits."

"Say less." I disconnect the call and make a U-turn, heading back to the private airstrip I just left a few hours ago. My luggage is still in my car since I never made it home. And what I don't have, I'll buy. Sending Zi and Mila a quick text, letting them know I was out and would touch base soon.

"Fuck this love shit." I sigh.

# Chapter 8

# Mila

We have arrived home from Vegas, trying to piece our lives together here in Cadence. Where do we live? How do our daily schedules mesh or clash? When do I meet his family? Oh God! His family. What will they think of me? I hardly know anything about this man. And nothing about them really. How will he handle my lupus? We will experience that real soon because I am most certainly at the beginning of a flare up and I have no one to blame but myself. I partied like a mutha effin' rock star over the last week. And the week before was filled with work stress, shopping, etc., while trying to prepare for the holiday celebrations.

Gazing down at my exquisitely designed serene blue, pear-shaped aquamarine ring, it's got to be at least five carats, surrounded by a halo of brilliant round-cut diamonds, micro-pavé set that amplifies the aquamarine's cool fire without overwhelming its presence.

And the band! It's a twisted shank platinum design with two diamond-adorned strands cross in a fluid, infinity-like shape. Bleu truly outdid himself. And I couldn't be happier.

When Bleu comes in the door from the garage, I run to him and hug him as tightly as I can.

"Hey, hey, Sweet." He kisses the top of my head, steadying us so we don't fall.

"I can get used to a greeting like this after a workday." He chuckles.

We are at his house tonight. Now standing in the kitchen, holding one another in silence. He lifts me up and I hug his neck tighter.

"You good, baby? What's goin' on?" He bends his neck trying to see my face.

Avoiding his eyes, I nod my head in the crook of his neck. I don't have the words to speak. My heart is so full and overjoyed. "I love you, Bleu," I whisper.

"I love you too, Mila. Is everything good?" I nod again into his neck.

He sets me on my feet, towering over me. He lifts my chin with his index finger. "Hey, where does that head and those eyes belong, love?" he chides gently.

Taking a deep breath, "I'm having a hard time being away from you all day now after last week," I admit. I'm doing what Nicole said today in therapy. Normalizing my emotions and expressing them. We are implementing a new framework in my therapy, Dialectical Behavior Therapy or DBT, which helps one with Mindfulness, Distress Tolerance, Emotion Regulation, and Interpersonal Effectiveness. All of which I need terribly. Me and emotions equal disaster and devastation. I don't want to continue that life. I want better and different, so I am *doing* better and different.

"I'm glad it's not just me then. I wanted to call you, text you, and FaceTime you all day today. I didn't though. I don't want to scare you away. And I know you have other things to do outside of me," he confesses.

"Baby, I want that, too! Let's make a deal, k? How about we normalize doing what we feel without overthinking it?"

"Uhh..."

"Ok, hear me out. We won't get crazy with it and if we do, we communicate and reign it back in. What I mean is, this is new to the both of us. Our marriage is *our* journey to create. Yeah, there are some guidelines but for the most part, the details are ours as we see fit. I don't like to cook all the time, and you don't mind cooking. But you hate cleaning the bathroom, and I don't mind. We don't subscribe to gender and/or societal roles, we do what works in our household. What do you think?"

"Ok, I see you, Sweet. I like that a lot. We have to promise though, to be easy on the judgment, use soft words in our communication, and pledge to understand before anger."

"Oooo, I love that. Gimme some, Mr. Patrick, we make a great team." I pucker my lips for a kiss.

"That's whatcho' mouf *say*, let's see whatcho mouf *do*." He starts walking me backward out of the kitchen.

"Naw, dawg, it goes with you to introduce me to your family and announce our marriage. That's what my mouf do."

He busts out laughing, "That's right Mrs. Patrick, keep yo' man on track, 'cause you know I'll stay in them guts."

I lick my tongue out at him and his nasty ass grabs it with his teeth then begins sucking on it, kissing me in a way that makes me decide anything we have on the agenda for tonight can wait until I love on my husband.

***

Showering after our "I missed you all day" sex session, Bleu inquires about what my dream wedding looks like.

"I mean, I'm not mad. Maybe disappointed because for as long as I can remember, I've wanted a destination wedding with family and friends. Something that screams decadence and romance. I saw a video of the most beautiful lagoon in the Cook Islands and when I close my eyes, I can feel the warmth from the sun as it slowly begins its late afternoon descent. Soft, delicate shades of cream, blue, and orange cascading from the sky, sea, and flowers to the wedding party's garb."

"It has to take place at the exact time, golden hour just like back home in Chicago before the sun sets and the world glows in warm amber tones. Casting what looks like liquid gold across the water's surface and bathing everything it touches in honeyed light. Ooooo!" I smile with my eyes closed, while reminiscing on past drives around Lake Shore Drive. Bleu continues to slowly wash me, listening intently.

"A simple altar at the water's edge, with soft, white sheer drapes flowing in the gentle breeze, soft music playing. Candles, some nicely decorated chairs for guests. Well, your family since I don't have any." I pause.

"Go on, I'm listening." He pulls my hair back behind my ear.

"While I don't hate getting married to you after meeting just a week ago," I roll my eyes and smile, "...doing so on a drunken night in Vegas was definitely not how I envisioned getting married."

"I feel you."

"We got the romance part right though." I give him a soft smile. "JaCaryous, none of that takes away from how I feel about you or dictate our future. I don't know what I'm doing or have any healthy, positive role models, but I promise you I will try my hardest to love you as you deserve and make this marriage the best decision you ever made."

"Damn, Mi. You promise a nigga all that?"

"Yep. I wish I could remember what was said and done in that chapel."

"Well don't worry, we will make new and coherent memories that you'll never forget. We gone be like the oldies in *The Notebook*." He grins.

"The movie?"

"Yep."

"Nooooo. They went years apart and unhappy."

"Girl, I said *the oldies*. We are going to have all the good years of growing and loving each other as unconditionally as possible."

"Now that, I can get with." I reach over and kiss his cheek.

# Chapter 9

# BLEU

Not even a week after returning from Vegas, duty calls and I've been gone four days. What was supposed to be a quick overnight business trip became this never-ending slew of back-to-back meetings. I miss my wife. Exhausted as fuck, I catch a red-eye trying to make it home before Mila wakes up.

It feels like I'm messing up. It's bad enough I had to leave unexpectedly a week after we returned from Vegas. And she's in the beginning stages of a flare up. I've never experienced one with her before. As much as she prepares me, I also know that they aren't the same all the time. I pray this one is not a bad one.

I quickly nip that in the bud. I make the conscious decision to not start my marriage off this way. I will profusely apologize to Mila and set the tone for future company meetings. I will always make time for my wife. Those who have differing opinions are welcome to move around.

*** 

After what feels like an eternity, I make it home. I toe off my shoes and slide through the hallway like I don't belong in my own damn home. She's in bed, facing the wall, blanket tucked to her chin. Still. Peaceful. But her energy? I feel the absence of me in the room like it's waiting on an apology. Or maybe it's just my guilt.

I sit at the edge of the bed, careful not to shift the mattress. Just close enough to breathe her in. I can't resist the need to feel her, so I slip in between the sheets, cradling her body, sniffing her hair and the base of her neck. God, I missed her so much.

*"Mi..."* I whisper, voice low, throat tight. She doesn't move. It's ok. I don't need her to. Glad to be home and home with my wife in my arms, my body fully relaxes, and I drift off to sleep.

It feels like my head touched the pillow two minutes ago when I hear my phone ringing. It's my mom. I answer it, doing my best to keep up with the conversation while fighting sleep.

"Yeah, Ma. I know. Well, we will let you know. This past week has been a lot for Mila. She's not feeling the best. And I haven't been here to help her. Let her rest and then I'll call you to get something set up so you can officially meet her. Yes, Ma, a family dinner. Ok. We love you, too."

"Girl, you got you a Cadence fan club and they haven't even met you yet." I turn over and see Mila curled into a tight ball under the covers.

Since we've returned from Vegas, Mila is struggling a bit getting back up to speed and this flare up isn't helping.

I know Sweet believes I'm super positive and motivating. I am for the most part, but I'm scared as shit of this Lupus bullshit and I now see first-hand how it tears her down. Her fatigue is so severe, she can't even lift her head from her pillow. And the pain...God, the pain, I don't know how she tolerates it. I don't think I could. She describes it as feeling like someone is grinding her bones. Man! This girl is strong as shit.

Mi has been and will always be my now, my then, my forever. Mila became mine before I even knew who she was and vice versa. My baby hasn't had the best life experiences, but she keeps moving forward. And if I can make her life easier in any shape, form, or fashion then I do and will.

I know she's scared. She's scared for her but for me as well. This fear is what I'm determined to help her conquer so she can live her best life as Mrs. Mila Nicole Patrick. The night we got married in Vegas was the absolute best night of my life. Mila was so carefree and living in the moment. No pain, no worries, no concerns. My only regret is that my family wasn't there, BUT I plan to rectify that by giving Mila the wedding of her dreams. One where she will be 100% coherent and remember every detail and my family will be a part of the planning and participation.

"Mmmm..."

I reach over and gently kiss her cheek. Watching and waiting as I do to see what she needs. She groans again and slowly tries to turn over in the bed. I see a tear shimmer above her cheek beneath her lashes. Her eyes remain closed. Her groans turn into soft whimpers.

"Sweet," I whisper softly, wiping the tears that are a constant stream on her face now.

"Tell me what you need, baby. What can I do to help you, Mi?"

"Bleu?"

"Yes, Sweet. It's me. Stop trying to open your eyes. I'm here, let me be your sight."

"It hurrrtttss, Bleu."

"Ok, baby, I got you. Can I touch you?"

"Yesss. I'm sorry." She cries softly.

"For what, love? Being human?"

She can't even answer. Her face scrunches up in pain.

"I'm here, baby, tell me what hurts, and I'll rub some CBD cream on you."

"All of it, Bleu. My legs feel like my bones are in a meat grinder." She groans.

"I gotchu. Gimme a sec." I get the travel size heating pad from my bag, her CBD cream, Tramadol, and water then return to the bed. She's in the fetal position now, groaning and silently crying. I can't even hold her, this shit is ripping my heart to shreds. Knowing that I can't take her physical pain away.

Thank God her eyes are closed, I wipe my tears from her thighs. I can't front like this shit is easy to witness.

"Alright, Mi, first, I'm going to slightly elevate your head to give you a Tramadol to help with the pain. Open your mouth, stick out your tongue a little bit, Sweet." I place the pill on her tongue. "Good girl. Ok swallow." I instruct her as I place the water bottle to her lips.

"Sweet, remind me to use these same instructions when you feel better." She makes a poor attempt to chuckle. That's what I need to see. I want to try and redirect her focus some to help her calm down. Her heart is beating so fast, it's got me shook.

"Ok, nasty girl, I'm gonna start at your pelvis and rub down each leg and foot slowly with the cream. I got the heating pad on the opposite leg, ok?"

"K." Her tears and whimpers are subsiding. I feel her heart rate slowing down.

We're quiet for a few minutes. "You don't have to turn over. I gotchu. I'm putting the heating pad on your right leg now and covering it and gonna rub your left leg and foot down the same way, ok?"

If I wasn't looking, I'd have missed the slight movement of her head. I softly sing Louis York & Anthony Hamilton's, *Alone A Lot,* swiping away the one tear on my cheek that escapes from my eye. This is my baby's life. *Our* life. I watch her wince and wonder if this was what pain looks like when it finally gets tired of being quiet. She wears emotional wounds like her second skin, now her body bears the burden, too. I just want to be a soft landing for her no matter the issue or the problem. I know I rushed things by wife-ing her like within literal days of meeting her, but ain't that the romantic shit the she be reading about and wishing for from a nigga?

I finish rubbing Sweet's leg and foot down. I place the heating pad across them, beneath the covers to keep the heat in, hopefully bringing her comfort. She's fallen back to sleep thankfully.

I remove the cream and pills from the bed while looking at my heartbeat in human form as she finally begins to rest.

"Mi...You think I'm saving you. But it's you, Sweet. You're the one saving *me,*" I whisper as I climb into bed behind her. I need to feel her touch but don't want to move or wake her, so I gently place her hand in mine, intertwining our fingers and immediately, sleep straight snatches my ass.

But not before I hear her whisper, "We are saving each other, Jay."

***

"Morning, babe." Mila yawns, covering her mouth, not wanting to share her morning breath.

"Morning, Sweet." I move her hand from her mouth, licking her lips, and plunge my tongue into her mouth.

"Bleu!" Shrieking my name while trying to close her mouth and move me away from her at the same time.

I roll onto my back, bringing her with me. She nestles her face in my neck.

"Mi?"

"Yeah?"

I exhale, eyes lock on hers. Now is as good a time as any to have this discussion with her. There are promises... easy on the judgment, use soft words in our communication, and pledge to understand before anger. I hope she remembers.

"Can you hold me with your eyes for a second? I need to let this breathe."

"Of course, baby. What is it? What's wrong, Bleu?"

"I ain't tryna mess this up."

"Mess what up?" she asks, fear evident in her eyes.

I gesture between us. "This. You. Me. I just... I need to say this right. You got me?"

She nods slowly, not saying a word. I can feel her tremble slightly. Holding me closer as if that's possible, she whispers, "Whatever you need, love."

I inhale deeply.

"Sweet, I love you more than the air I breathe. I know I pursued the shit outta you. All gas—"

"No brakes at all, nigga." She chuckles lowly.

"You're worth it, though. I couldn't risk some lame trying to take what is mine. With that being said, Mi, I can't help but feel... afraid about this Lupus."

Instinctively, I tighten my hold on her. Just as I knew she would, she immediately starts struggling, trying to remove herself from my grasp.

"Mila, stop!"

Watery eyes look back at me. "I need, *we*, need to be able to hold space for one another when there are some unattractive words that need to be shared. I specifically asked you, *"Can you hold me with your eyes for a second? I need to let this breathe."* And your response was, *"Of course, baby. What is it? What's wrong, Bleu?"*

"I know it's instinct for you to run but you've got to stop, Sweet. We won't make it by running. Either of us. And I know that you know this. Do you think I want to you to feel unsafe? I would never intentionally hurt you, baby. I'd bleed so you won't hurt."

"Look at me, Sweet. You feel me?"

She nods, "I'm sorry, Bleu."

"You don't have to be sorry, love. I just want us to be on the same page and equally committed to making this work. Remember we DBT-ing this thing. Easy on the judgment, use soft words in our communication, and pledge to understand before anger."

Grabbing my face and peering into my eyes so deeply, she says, "I am. I am committed, baby. I'm scared, too. But I have never wanted anything more besides wanting my family to still be alive. I'm so in love with you, JaCaryous. Yeah, I know things happened quickly but Bleu... you answer a call my soul's been whispering for a long time."

"Mila, baby, I'm so glad—"

"Wait, Bleu, let me finish."

"Sweet?" My body freezes.

"JaCaryous. I think we need—"

"No, Mila. Don't."

"Baby, this is not easy, but I need, we need to..."

"Don't do this, Mila... please, baby. Just hold on. Let *me* finish. It's terrifying watching you suffer, baby." My voice cracks as I pull her closer to me. If I hold her close, she won't let me go. I can make all of this go away.

"I know, but everything just moved so quickly. We got caught up in the excitement of it all. And it's ok, baby." She moves back and places my face between her hands.

"Sweet, Mila, baby, please." I close my eyes. The pain feels like I can't breathe. I place her hand beneath mine on my chest and kiss her. Slow at first. I need to make her stop talking.

She pulls away from me, "Bleu, you know I can't think straight when you do this to me."

"Sweet, just let me love you. Let me show you. Mila, please don't end us before we get started." I whisper, swiping the tears angrily from my face. I can't believe we are back here.

"Baby, no, don't cry." She whispers as she kisses my tears away.

"I'm not saying we need to divorce or get an annulment, but I am saying that we need a little time apart."

"NO! Don't do this, Sweet."

"Bleu! Listen! Baby, I love you. I love you enough to hear you. I see you, JaCaryous. I see the struggle and the fear in your eyes. I saw it when the flare up first began. And again when you returned from your business trip. I know your heart. You want to support me. You want to love me through the pain. You just aren't sure you can. And baby, that's ok. I love you and us enough to say the hard things you're afraid to say."

I drop my head as the tears continue falling. I'm so ashamed. I'm angry at myself for not being strong enough to care for my wife in the capacity she needs. I'm sad that I feel like I continuously fail her. I'm hurt that she wants to give me space and doesn't want to stay in the trenches with me. She thinks she's doing the right thing but nothing could be more wrong.

I don't know how long I stay in this headspace but when I look up, Mila is nowhere to be found.

"Sweet!!" I frantically make my way throughout the house yelling her name, only to be met with silence. I call her phone repeatedly until it eventually goes straight to voicemail.

"Arrgghhh!" I yell into the abyss. I have no one to blame but myself. I call her again, preparing to leave a voicemail. *"Mi, baby. It's me. Come home, baby. I need you, Mi. Please."* My voice breaks. I end the call and lie my head back on the sofa.

I jolt awake, knowing exactly where she went. Rushing to get presentable, I grab my keys, wallet, and phone, exiting the door to the waterfront.

# Chapter 10
# Mila

S eeing him so broken shattered my heart and my dreams of a happy marriage into a million pieces. I don't know much about marriage or relationships for that matter but I do know not to involve outside parties. So as much as I wanted to call one of my girls or Whyte, I didn't. This is something to be worked out with my husband.

My husband. Who am I right now? Hell, who is he? What are we even doing? My husband. This man adores me. I think what hurts the most is that his words mirror my concerns. He is supposed to be the strongest and most steadfast between us two. But is that fair to put that all in him? What if he decides one day, this... *I* am too much for him? Would I survive that? Could I survive that?

My text chimes, interrupting my thoughts. *Ding. Ding*... what the?

> **Bleu:** *You know this is my favorite view of you.*

> **Bleu**: *Hey pretty girl, why so sad? What do I tell you about looking down, raise your head and show that beautiful face, Mi.*

I raise my head, pull my shoulders back, and openly wipe my face.

> **Bleu:** *There she is. Come to me, love.*

He doesn't have to say it twice, I instinctively know where he is, just as he knew where to find me. I turn my head slightly to the right and I see him walking in my direction, so I begin walking in his direction. I pick up the pace and before I know it, I'm running into his arms.

"Whoa! Did you miss me, Mi?"

I just want to take a second and immerse myself in him. Feeling the side of his face, his locs, his shoulders and back, the lines of his tattoos. I kiss the spot right beneath his ear and feel him shudder and brick up simultaneously. I burrow my face in his neck as I try climbing into his skin. Every breath I take is Bleu. My God, I love this man. Fear or not, I know in this moment, I will take the chance and love him while letting him love me. Praying we make it.

"Huh, Sweet?" He tries pulling away to see my face, but I need to be one with him. I am not ready to interrupt this sensual, sensory moment with words, so I hold him closer, attaching myself to him like a spider monkey.

I nod my head in the crook of his neck, still holding him so tight.

"Why, my love?" I mumble into his neck.

He lets out a deep sigh and I feel his shoulders relax, even though he is still holding me up, hugging me tightly with one arm, the other beneath my ass, as my legs are wrapped around his waist. I'm anxious as hell waiting on him to say something.

"What took you so long to find me, Bleu?"

Look down at me with those beautiful blue eyes and that sexy smirk, his facial expression tells me I was never lost.

"Sweet, first, let me apologize for upsetting you. I am so sorry, Mila. I love you, baby, and don't want to ever be without you and I don't ever, ever want to give you a reason to be sad or cry. You do not deserve that.

"Hey, can I see your face?"

I shake my head. He tries pulling us apart but I can't let go. I'm really trying to break the habit of running. I just need a few more seconds of him anchoring me, us.

"Just finish please. I need to feel you like this for a while longer, ok?" I whisper in neck.

He nods and continues, "You love me, Sweet?"

I nod my head.

"I need to hear you say it, my love."

"I love you more than life itself, JaCaryous." It sounds muffled because my face is still buried in his skin.

He chuckles lightly. "It wasn't too long ago, I had to chase you down, now you're trying to climb into my shirt with me."

"And am." I sniffle.

We both laugh a bit while I slowly release my grip on him.

"Thank you, baby. You was stranglin' a nigga." He kisses my cheek.

Releasing his midsection, I unwrap my legs and slowly slide down his front, purposefully slowing down on his dick. I lift my eyes when I hear him inhale sharply.

"Fuck, Sweet."

"Hmm? What I do, bae?" I blink my eyes slowly, innocently.

"Girl. Cmon!"

"Wait!" I'm laughing so hard at him dragging me behind him rushing us to my SUV.

"Nah, you want this dick and Ima give it to you. Bring ya' ass, Mi." I can barely breathe while trying to keep up, being so turned on, and laughing at his crazy ass. He pushes me into the backseat of my SUV, closing the door, ripping my thong smooth off seemingly in one motion, diving head first into my essence. Lawd, I'm glad I'm wearing a skirt.

"Ah, baby!"

"Mmm hmm, bring yo' lil' short ass here." He gripped my hips with his hands and hooked my legs in the crook of his elbows, locking me in.

How is he talking in my pussy? The hell.

"Less talkin', more eatin'."

Those blue eyes find my brown ones, letting me know the challenge has been accepted.

"Bet."

"Unh Bleu, ooo! Oh. My. God. JaCaryous!"

He's licking and slurping my pussy so good. He wets his finger in my juices and sticks it slowly but with mad intention in my asshole. *In, slurp, out, long slow lick, in, slurp, out, long slow lick.* This cadence is making me lose my mind. I can't comprehend. I can only feel and the feelings are so intense, this nigga is on a mission, fah real.

I feel like I lose track of time but my body didn't. The way JaCaryous is putting in work is detrimental to my damn sanity. I don't know how many orgasms I've experience in this short amount of time, I feel like I blacked out at some point.

I'm back to reality as I watch him watch me with this shit eatin' grin on his face. He removes my legs from his arms. His sweats and boxer briefs are around his ankles and his thick, golden brown rod is pointing out and upward.

I look at his dick, then up at him, licking my lips like Tom the cat on that old cartoon *Tom and Jerry* when he sees Jerry the mouse.

"Uh huh." He pulls me into his lap, lifting me and slowly placing me down the length of his dick. My back to his front. He slaps my left ass cheek. Then says in a sexy, low tone, "You know what I like."

I brace each of my hands on his thighs, bend forward a bit, feet planted on the floor of the truck, and go to work.

"Ah, shit, girl! You know I love you, right?"

"Mmm hmm."

"Gat damn, Mi, wait a second, shit!"

What he say that for, my goal was to make this nigga come hard and fast. Two can play that game. Watching the clock on the dash, one minute and 19 seconds later...

"Fuuuckkk, Mila! I love you, Sweet! Shit!" Growling, he stiffens and shoot so much cum in me, it beckons another breath, snatching an orgasm from me. He didn't just shoot up the club, it was a full on massacre in that bitch.

Leaning back on his chest trying to catch my breath, "Bleu. We didn't use protection, baby."

"Is that a bad thing?"

"I don't know, is it?" Eyebrows knitted together, I ask.

"Well, we have not had that conversation as a married couple."

"Ok, let's have it." Bleu shrugs his shoulders nonchalantly.

"Now?"

"Why not, you don't want my babies, love?"

"Don't do that. That's not fair." I begin moving out of his grasp so I can redress.

"No. Stop, JaCaryous. Don't kiss on me. You distract me too much. Bleu!"

"Bet. Can we just go home first and discuss this later? We gotta get ready for dinner with the family," he says while grabbing napkins and wipes from the console to clean us, fixing my clothes, then his.

"No. Depending on what you have to say, *we* may not have a home to return to." I look at him pointedly, raising one eyebrow. Judging by the stormy look on his face, I may have overstepped. He didn't like my
statement one bit.

"Mila, I'm going to get out of your truck. You're going to get out of the backseat of your truck. Then you're going to walk around the front of your truck and hop your little, short ass in the driver's seat, and wait for me, then you *will* follow me HOME. No stops. No detours. Straight to *our* home. You hear me?"

Oh! He put the *deep* bass in his voice.

"Mmm hmm." I hummed, rolling my eyes. How am I horny again and I still got this nigga's legacies trying to run down my thighs?

"As a matter of fact, gone on and head to the house. I'll be right behind you. Be yo ass somewhere else and it's gone be one, feel me?"

I roll my eyes and get out of the truck, and he grabs me back in by the nape of my neck, turning me on so very much.

"I didn't hear you agreeing, Sweet. Now say, yes Daddy."

I bust out laughing, "Boy please. I heard you."

"Aight, play pussy and get fucked."

The hell does that even mean? He stalks his sexy ass over to what looks like a black Ducati motorcycle, hops on, starts it up, and puts on a helmet. I pull off and true to his word, he's right on my ass. Where'd he get a whole Ducati from?

Lord be with me, 'cause only You know what he is going to tell me.

# Chapter 11

# BLEU

Two days later, I held Honey off as long as I could without her popping up at our home. Hmm... *our* home. Mila and I haven't fully decided whose place we would reside in full time, but she was at mine more often than not. However, we did decide to build something new that

reflects both of our tastes. Of course, with her being Thee Interior Designer, she has carte blanche for everything except my office and mancave. And honestly, she will probably design and decorate those too, who am I kidding?

"Now, that we've gotten—hold on, this is Mama. I've missed three of her calls and she is not gonna be happy."

She tries to extricate herself from my grasp to give me privacy on my call, but I don't let her. Instead, I kiss her beneath the ear as I answer the phone.

"Hey, gorgeous."

"Don't you *hey gorgeous* me, my wayward son. Where are you? I thought you were coming by."

"I'm with your daughter-in-law right now, giving her some ack-right."

"Oh my God, Bleu! Hi, Mrs. Patrick. How are you?"

"Mila? How are you, sweetheart? I can't wait to finally meet you! My son has been calling you *my daughter-in-law* since we first saw you in Target." She chuckles.

Mila is blushing so hard. I pinch her cheek and place a wet, juicy kiss on her lips.

"Anyway, Ma. We will be over soon, and you can meet the new Mrs. Patrick. But I need to run and I promise I'll call you back in a bit to have a real convo."

"Alright, son. Mila! I look forward to hugging your face real soon!"

"Same here, Mrs. Patrick."

"No ma'am. Mrs. Patrick is my mother-in-law and now you." Mama snickers in her signature way.

"You can call me Ma, Mama, Jessinia, or Honey. If those don't work, we can come up with something."

"Ok...Ma?" She's so cute when she's blushing and shy.

I hear Mama clapping excitedly. "Ooooo! I got me a daughter for real y'all!" Laughing, I told her we'd be by shortly and I end the call.

"Alright, Sweet. I know, we, well, I came in hot... don't roll your eyes at me, lil one. Anyway, as I was saying. We need to put in our time getting to know the basics at least about each other. Whatcha think?"

"Unh! Sweet, wait a minute, baby! What's all this? I like it, but what's happening?" As soon as I asked what she thought about my idea, she tackles me onto the bed, smothering my face in kisses. And of course, my

mans is uber reactive to all things Mila Nicole.

"JaCaryous." Kiss. "I love that beautiful mind of yours." Kiss, kiss, kiss. "That's been one of my concerns."

"One of—"

"Shhhh. Focus, baby. You already know it was difficult to let go of control and just *be*. Just *feel*. But I wanted to. I **want** to. I wanted to say, *fuck it and be with Bleu*. So, I did. I did so, not knowing much about you or your family. All I knew for sure was that I want and need

JaCaryous Kristoff Patrick, past, present, and future. For you to initiate conversation to make sure we get to know one another, makes me wanna have all yo' babies!"

Hearing her say she want a nigga's babies got my dick about to detonate.

She kisses all over my face again. "Challenge accepted, Mi." I flip her lil' ass over quickly and enter her carefully but uncovered...again.

"Bleuuuuu..... baby. Oh my...shiiiiittttt! Wait, baby, you so deep. You don't have a con—"

I slap her hand off my stomach, "That's what you want, Mi? You want me to stop?"

"Nooo," she whines. "It's just so, fuck, it's so good. What are you doing to me?!"

"Gimme that shit, Mrs. Patrick. You said you want a nigga's babies, I'm giving you whatchu want." I continue deep stroking the shit outta her while playing with her clit, making her moan and coo. Imprinting on her very soul. Our rhythm begins to quicken. Her shit is so

slippery from her raining on my shit, I feel that nut hit my spine like an electric volt. Shit feels like lightning is traveling down the backs of my legs, I literally hear the bones in my hands and toes crack as my kids make their way into their new home... their mama.

"Fuuuuccccckkkk!"

"Oh shit, JaCaryous... I love you!" she exclaims, releasing and welcoming simultaneously.

Trying to catch our breaths, I embrace her and roll us over to a dry spot on the bed and kiss each of her closed eyes.

"I love you too, Mrs. Patrick. And just know you should be careful telling me the desires of your heart because I venture to give you your every wish and desire." I kiss her stomach and say, "Welcome home, son."

"The fuck?!" she screeches.

"Heh, heh, heh."

\*\*\*

"Alright, what I am walking into over here in the Patrick household. Set the scene for me. Anything I should be aware of? Shouldn't say, do, or eat? What if your mom, sorry Honey, doesn't like me? Or your dad? Or your brother? What do I call your dad?"

"Breathe, Mi, dang." I rub her thigh, attempting to calm her a bit.

"They will *all* love you like I do. By the way, have I told you how beautiful you look? I love making you blush. Put your hand on my thigh. I wanna feel you while I'm driving. This is my *preference*." I grin at her mischievously.

"I gotchu." She thinks she's so funny. Lightly strumming her fingers up my thigh, making my dick twitch.

"Aight. Get fucked in Honey's house." I laugh so hard at the way she snatches her hand from my crotch like her shit was on fire. I grab her hand and place it on my thigh, covering it with mine.

"You can call my dad Pops, Ephraim, or Mr. Patrick if that makes you more comfortable. He's just an older, slightly darker skin version of me. He's cool as a fan. And he's gonna love you, watch. And my brother, JJ or

John Jacob, is a couple years younger than me. He looks like me and Pops and has a dog named Bozo. I think he's still single, no kids."

"Oh yeah, don't trip on the house and stuff, my family is like a staple in the community and shit."

"What kind of declaration is that? What kind of staple?"

Pulling up to the security gate, I tap in my code. While waiting for the gate to open, her mouth drops open. Chuckling, I crook my index finger beneath her chin and close her mouth.

"Bleu, what kinda generational wealth is this? Are you rich? Are they rich? Are we rich?"

Driving up the winding driveway, I park and shut off the truck, leaving her in suspense as I jump out of the truck to open her door. "Cmon, lil one."

I watch her glide out of the truck, all five foot two of her—soft curves wrapped in sun-kissed light brown skin. Her hair falls just past her shoulders in waves of brown laced with hints of red, catching the light like a quiet flame. Those almond-shaped eyes, rich as caramel, hold a gaze that lingers in awe. Her lips—full, kissable, dangerous. And that delicate nose, pierced with a sapphire stud, gives her just enough edge to make desire curl low in my stomach. It's the matching sapphire tongue ring and those damn waist beads she wears that makes me wanna push her up against the truck and fuck her senseless.

I block her path and place a slow, gentle kiss on her lips. "I love you, Mila. Thank you for being my everything."

Her hands fly to her mouth and tears fill her eyes, "Oh, JaCaryous. No. Thank *you*."

The front door flies open and Honey steps out onto the porch, arms open wide, "Hi, babies."

"Hey, Ma." I hug her then bring Mila in front of me, "Ma, this is my wife, your daughter-in-law, Mila Patrick."

"Bleu, I'll be glad when you all finally do get married, maybe your dream will come true," she said, hugging Mila.

Mi looks back at me with a worried expression on her face.

"Cmon y'all, let's go in." I usher them into the house. "Where's Pops and JJ?" I ask my mom.

"They're in the den watching television. Your grandparents are here, too."

She's holding both of Mila's hands, grinning from ear to ear.

"Mila. You are beautiful." She gushes and hugs her again.

"Bleu, she's even more beautiful up close, in person."

"Ma, let her breathe." I snake in between them to take Mila's hands into mine, noticing she's beginning to look overwhelmed.

"Ok, ok."

Following Honey through the house I watch Mila taking it all in. I already know she's going to have a lot to say when we leave.

"Mrs. Pat-, um, Honey..." Mila reaches out to touch my mom's arm. She extends her hand to her, handing her a bottle of Cadence Kiss Reserve. Mama looks at the label and her eyes dart towards mine. I give her a subtle shake of the head. She grabs Mila again in an embrace.

"You're so kind, Sugarfoot. This will go perfect with the lamb we're serving tonight. You choose this one or did JaCaryous suggest it?"

"No ma'am. I'm trying to up my game and learn more about the different wines and seeing which ones, if any, that I like. And I really like this one. I hope y'all would, too. Oh, Bleu, I left the box in the car. Would you get it for me, please?"

"Of course, Sweet. I'll get it after I introduce you to everyone, if that's ok?" She nods her head in agreement, turning her attention back to my mom.

"Sweetheart, you're going to fit right in." Honey looks at me and winks as we round the corner to the family room where everyone else is congregating.

I pull Mila closer to me and say, "Everyone, this is my heartbeat, Mrs. Patrick, or you can call her Mila. It's a bunch of y'all so be easy with my baby and don't overwhelm her."

"Boy, hush," my dad says, moving me out of the way, embracing Mila. "Nice to meet you, Mila. I'm this one's dad, Ephraim Patrick. Or Pops. Whichever you're more comfortable with calling me."

"Nice to meet you too, Mr.- uh, Pops." She ducks her head bashfully.

"Alright, alright, unhand my sister-in-law. Hey, Boo. I'm JJ. Bleu's one and only brother and faithful sidekick. You're even more beautiful up close." He gave her a quick side hug and me a thumbs up. Mila looks back at me confused because first Honey said it, now JJ.

"Give us a sec. Grandparents, get ready cuz we coming in hot when we return." They all giggle and I direct Mila into the kitchen to give her a quick breather. I gently pull her into a hug. Pulling her face up so her gaze can meet mine, "You good?"

She looks like she's going to cry, "Yeah. It's a lot at once. I forgot what it's like to be in a real family."

Hugging her closer to me, chest to chest so her heartbeat can sync to mine. She's so short, I have to squat down to do it. "It's ok, Sweet. They just wanna love on you is all. But we will do this in your timing. You just be you, unapologetically. Ok?"

She nods her head in the crook of my neck. I can feel her relax as our heartbeats sync. I pull back into my full height but continue embracing her until she lets go. "You ready?"

"Yep." She smiles at me lovingly. "Don't forget the box in the car, ok?"

"I gotchu." Gat damn, that smile. It's a battery pack to my soul. Soon as I see it, my chest heats up—feels like sun rays beaming straight through my ribs. Grabbing my hand, we head back to the family room.

"Alright, who's next in line?" I clap and rub my hands together.

"Oh Bleu! You are such a character." Nana wraps her arms around my middle, all five feet of her. A little pixie of a woman—barely a hundred pounds soaking wet. Sweet as pie, but you don't ever wanna land on her bad side. That woman's got a bite like a viper.

"Mila, your twin in height over here is my Nana, Jeaux, my mom's mom and this gentle giant is my Pop Pop, my mom's dad, Ace Saint James."

"Well, aren't you a beauty! Good job, Jay," Ace winks at me and pinches Mila's cheek.

"Move over, Ace, we short gals gotta stick together." Nana grabs Mila's hands in hers.

Mila giggles and relaxes even more.

"Hi, Nana. Hi, Ace. It's really nice to meet you."

"Our turn!" Sassy twirls Mila in her direction.

"Well, hey now!" Mila laughs, surprised, but smiling at Sassy's energy.

"Hey, Sweetpea, I'm Sassy and this is Conwell, we call him Boss, and we are Bleu's daddy's folks." They both grab Mila up into a big bear hug. Mila looks like she's been a part of our family for years. Standing back, watching all of this unfold, confirms what I've known all

along. I made the right choice in following my heart and pursuing Sweet the way I did. I was crazy to ever think anything different.

Handing the Saint James dessert truffle box from the car Mila asked me to grab for her while she's in a conversation with Honey, Sassy, and Nana.

"Baby, can you put this in the kitchen for me, please?" She pulls my chin down so she can kiss my lips.

That shit got me harder than cement. "Sweet," I bend down to her ear and kiss right below it, "Baby... I want you so bad right now." I whisper in her ear.

"Bleu, you do see us too, right?" Honey asks, instigating.

"Mmhmm."

Mila's eyes meet mine, she says low enough only for me to hear, " I gotchu." Slightly grazing across the front of my pants as she turns back to her conversation with the ladies.

"Shiiiiiitttttt." I pull her back close to me, her back to my front and sway side to side so she can feel just how hard she's made me.

My mom catches my glance.

"Jay, go down to the cellar and get another bottle of Reserve please." She smirks and shakes her head. "And let the girl breathe." She winks.

\*\*\*

Mila leans over and whispers, "Is dinner like this *every* Sunday?"

"Yep. Embrace your new normal, Sweet." I tease her, grinning.

"So, your grandparents' last name is Saint James, like the name on the wine bottle and truffle desserts? The same Saint James from the Valley? That vineyard in the Valley is divine. I love their tasting events!" She whisper yells, not giving me a chance to answer any of her questions.

"First, I need you to breathe, Sweet. Second, yes, *our* grandparents are the proud owners of the Saint James Winery & Resort along with some other properties in Cadence. My cousins Poiré, Corqué, Sommé, Sémillon, & Zoëra Saint James run it. Poiré is the Sommelier and Zoëra is the chocolatier. You may have met her when you picked up the truffles and wine for dessert."

"Oh my God, baby! I've married into Cadence Royalty?!" she shouts, wide eyed, taking in everything and everyone milling around the dining room.

By now, I'm full-on belly laughing. "Cadence Royalty, Mi? Sure, I guess. You don't know the half of it though."

"Married?! JaCaryous Kristoff Patrick! I know damn well I didn't just hear Mila say she's *married* into Cadence Royalty?!" Honey fusses.

Mila looks like she is trying to become one with her chair. She is mortified. I look over at her and grab and kiss her hand. "It's ok, Mi." I reassure her.

"Ma..."

"No, Bleu, let me." Mila stops me. She stands to address the table. I stand alongside of her.

"Yes, Hon- Mrs. Patrick. JaCaryous and I apparently got married the night of July 4th when we were in Vegas."

"Bleu!" Nana sighs with tears in her eyes.

"Nana, wait. Let us explain," I interject.

"Listen, no one was more surprised that we were married than I was." Bleu and I look at each other and laugh. He kisses my forehead.

"We will explain all that as well. But please don't be upset. We were coming here today, not only for me to meet you but to announce our nuptials... aaannddd to discuss having a real and *agreed upon* marital ceremony."

"Ma, Nana, Sassy, guys, I love Mila."

"Ja—"

"Yes, it seems like it's quick. Technically, it kinda was but I fell in love with Sweet, what Mi, about a year ago? Ma and JJ, y'all were with me the first time I saw her in Target. I told you then she was Mrs. Patrick."

"You did, JaCaryous, but to go off and secretly get married without family?" Honey says dejectedly.

"Honey, I understand your disappointment, and I knew I'd have to face the family firing squad, which I'm more than happy to do. If you'd allow me the floor, I'll explain and then you can fire away."

She looks between me and Mila. Mila's eyes silently ask my mom for permission.

My dad corrals Mom to give me a few minutes to finish explaining. I kiss Sweet's temple.

"Ok, where was I? Oh, yeah, I saw her after seeing her in Target from time to time throughout Cadence. I even met her once at the Café and put her on notice **then**. As fate would have it, about a week ago, the day I touched down in Cadence, this angel walks right in front of my vehicle like God himself delivered her to me personally."

"See why I had to marry him?" she grins, starry eyed.

"Ha! Funny, Sweet. Anyway, y'all know July 4th is commemorative in more ways than one around here. When the Vegas opportunity presented itself, it was like divine intervention. Free flight on a private jet, dope ass suite, Mi had agreed to be my girl..."

"Your *girl*, JaCaryous. Not your *wife*."

"Well....after a few drinks and whispering sweet nothings in Sweet's ear, we were on the strip, then we were in the chapel. I may or may not have orchestrated the entire night. Mila agreed in the moment to legally become my wife and soooo... she is now."

"Granted, she didn't remember any events of the night before until the next morning when she found this beautiful wedding set on her hand," I lift her hand for everyone to see the ring.

"...but she loves me and *wants* to be Mrs. Patrick."

"I think he *love bombed* me, for real." Mila tries to lighten the mood, jokingly.

"Mila, really?" I ask, pretending to be slighted.

While Mila is laughing at her own joke, I kneel in front of her and say, "Mi...I feel like I took something from you. A moment you should've had—one you *deserve*. I would never cheat you out of anything that sacred.

Especially not love. Not us. So in front of the people who

love us, probably you more than me now — let me do this right. Will you marry me...again?"

All the ladies gasp and wipe tears from their eyes. The fellas sit up on the edge of their seats, waiting for Mila's answer.

I'm grinning like a loon waiting on the answer I see in her eyes. She understands how important it is for my family to be a part of this moment. Besides, what woman wouldn't like three proposals?

"JaCaryous, Bleu, thank you, baby. Thank you for giving me everything I didn't even know I need. And yes, baby, I will marry you...again."

I jump up and swing her around, planting a juicy, wet kiss on her kissable lips. The family is in the background celebrating. "Thank you, baby." I whisper in her ear.

"Look how happy this has made them."

"Anything for you, Bleu."

*** 

### Post Dinner Convo

"Mila, come sit between me and Nana." Sassy reaches out to her, clearing a space on the couch.

My mom walks with Mila into the den.

"So, Mi, I believe your words were, 'Let me find out you're Cadence Royalty.'" I imitate her little, soft voice, with my hand on my hip, acting like her when she talks.

She throws her head back laughing hard, tongue ring glistening. "No, JaCaryous. Those were not my exact words. You stay trying to imitate somebody."

Sassy interrupts, "Well, Mila. I wouldn't call us royalty per se, but we do have a healthy amount of blood, sweat, and tears imbedded into every square inch of soil that encompasses the city of Cadence. I am a direct descendant of the city's founder, Cadence Vertrees," Sassy declares proudly.

Mila's mouth drops open and her head is on a swivel, looking to everyone for confirmation. I lean over and whisper, "Flies, Sweet. You're determine to catch them." She quickly snaps her mouth shut.

Sassy continues, "I believe Bleu was beginning to explain to you how the Patricks and Saint Jameses are related. Here is a visual that may help with the convolution otherwise known as the Vertrees – Saint James' legacy. I don't expect you to remember any of this but you will receive your very own copy for your home and heirs to the legacy."

Mila's eyes are glossy when she speaks. "This is so overwhelmingly dope! And I am so very honored to be a part of this family. Show me, tell me, immerse me in all things Cadence, Sassy. I'm ready!" She squeals excitedly.

"Alright, baby girl. As my grandsons say, *Say Less!*" The room goes into an uproar with laughter.

Sassy opens this huge custom sized scroll with the found lineages for the Vertrees, Saint James, Patrick, and La Rue families.

"Whoooaaa..." Mila whispers, running her fingers lightly over the writing on the page. She looks like she's in a trance. We all quietly watch her embrace the spirits of the ancestors as she reads over their names. I

don't know how I could ever question being with her, even if it

was a fleeting moment. Watching her savor the history of not just *our* families but the Black history that has been made, she moves away quickly from the scroll so as not to allow tears to mar the page. I feel Honey

wrapping her arms around my middle and leaning her head

on my chest as best she can. It's more like my ribcage she's leaning into.

Sassy and Nana each have an arm around Mila, speaking softly in her ear. I watch as she takes in everything they're saying to her. I wouldn't be surprised if they weren't whispering ancestral prayers over her. Nana whispers something in Mila's ear. I see more tears falling as

Nana places her hand on Mila's stomach. Sassy places her hand on top of Nana's. Honey kneels in front of Mila, wiping her tears. They're all loving on her and affirming her. Not just with words but with love. Sassy speaks quietly to Mila again and her eyes meet mine. I whisper the words, *"I love you, Sweet."* And she blows me a quick kiss.

Man, I'm so glad that after the initial shock of hearing we were married, the ladies are still receptive and loving towards Mila. They embraced her and included her in whatever it is they do in the kitchen. As long as I could hear laughter and good cheer coming from her in that direction, everything was everything. I'd hate to have to two piece my mom and grannies. The visual made me chuckle to myself.

JJ claps a hand on my shoulder, nudging me in the direction of Ace, Boss, and Dad as they head out onto the deck for cigars and libations. "Cmon, nigga. She ain't gone dis-a-damn-ppear. Let's let the ladies welcome her into the fold in peace."

"It's crazy, right?"

"What's that?"

"How this is my life right now. Not even a week ago, I wasn't even a full resident of Cadence. And since then, I've met and married my soul."

"You mean soulmate?"

"Nah, nigga. That girl in there *is* me. In the best possible way."

"Yo... that sounds like some 'I wanna be in yo skin type shit.'"

"You stupid, bro. One day, you'll get it when it happens to you."

# Chapter 12

# BLEU

*O**n The Way Home***

"Why you so quiet, Sweet?"

"Mmm, no reason. Just taking in the scenery."

"I'm calling BS, Mila Patrick." Looking over at her she has the brightest, prettiest smile on her face.

"Do that again, baby, light up like that again."

"Call me Mila Patrick again."

"Mila Patrick, love of my life. Keeper of my soul."

Seeing her grin like that makes my heart skip a beat. "I know today was a lot. You good?"

"It was a whole lot! But in the absolute best way. Thank you, love muffin, for giving me a family."

"Love muffin?"

"No? Puddin' Cookie?"

"Puddin' Cookie? Sweet? You just went from bad to worse."

"Just wait, I'll find one for you."

"I know you will. How do you feel about being married into and now an intricate part of *"Cadence Royalty?"*

"That shit is so dope! When I was reading over the names and relationships, I swear I could feel the ancestors welcoming me in. The air was so heavy with tension. Not bad energy but like thick with presence. I had goosebumps. And the way Sassy and Nana were speaking in that moment. It was like they were speaking some sort of... I don't know. Like they were speaking over me but *to* me. Does that make sense? I know I sound crazy but I can't articulate it any better than that, Bleu. It was so surreal!"

"And when Nana asked if she could pray for my womb? For the healing. For the future. For the babies I've carried and the ones I haven't met yet, I was stunned. Then Sassy whispered and asked if she could pray over my womb, call the names only the ancestors know, call in the women who walked before me, and bless the space in me that holds what's not yet born, speak healing into the place they'd entrusted to me."

"I know you may think it's crazy but I swear I could feel like this... this... this energy flowing from within, Bleu!"

"I don't think you're cra-, wait... what did Nana say again?"

"She asked if she could pray for my womb. For the healing. For the future. For the babies I've carried and the ones I haven't met yet. Wait, that I've *carried*? Maybe I misheard what she's said. I've never been pregnant to my knowledge."

Bleu looks a little uneasy. "To your knowledge?"

"Yes. To. My. Knowledge. I have never been pregnant. Why the face and tone?"

"I mean, it sounds a bit ambiguous, don't you think?"

"Not really. What, you want me to say definitively that I have NEVER been pregnant, JaCaryous?"

"That would be nice, Mila Patrick. But only if it's the truth."

"Don't *Mila Patrick* me! It sounds like you're lowkey calling me a liar."

I grab her hand, "No, Mi." I sigh. "Just because I want to hear something in a specific way does not mean I think you're lying. This is just a part of meeting and getting married within a week, love."

We stop at a red light. I place the gear into the park position. I lean over in Mila's space, "Give me a kiss, pouty lips. Cmon. I won't let this get blown out of proportion. I apologize for offending you." I outline her lips with my tongue and she invites me in. We've forgotten that we are at a red light until the driver behind me honks their horn. I hit my hazard lights and wave them around. "I love you, Mi."

"I'm sorry, JaCaryous. And I love you, too. So damn much." She kisses the tip of my nose, my eyelids, and a quick peck on my lips. "Take me home so I can show you."

"Say muthafuckin' less!" I slam my hand on the hazard light button, throw the car in gear, and make this Porsche do what they say it can.

I'm locking the door behind us as Sweet peels us both out of our clothes. She sinks to her knees, pulls my dick out, and starts speaking to it in her own language.

I close my eyes, grip the doorframe, and send up a quiet *thank you* to the ancestors... for the sacred, undeniable power of the tongue. Her tongue.

Later, after we got cleaned up and lying in the bed, "I wonder what kind of sex did the ancestors have?"

"Mila? The fuck?" I crack up. "I would guess the same as we do. Where do you come up with this shit?

Hunching her shoulders, grinning, "Ion know. Like do you think Cadence was like, 'Pearson bring that dick in here?' Or was Mr. Johnson saying, 'My fairest Cadence, I would like permission to mount you now?'"

My side hurts and tears are rolling down my face at her voices and imitations. "Ahh, you a fool, Mi. Aye but leave my great, great, great grandmother outta that shit, real talk. I don't wanna think of her "getting mounted" or "dropping to her knees in her frock"."

"Her frock!?" She shrieks and we laugh for at least five more minutes. After we calm down, I turn over and face her, stroking her cheek with my hand.

"Yo, Sweet. *This*, this is what marriage is supposed to, nah scratch that, this is what **our** marriage *will* be like. I don't ever want the fun flame to die out. I love your wit and personality. It makes you uniquely you. Even when your smart ass mouth may piss me off."

"Oop!"

Kissing her into silence, I tell her I love her against her lips.

"I love your semi-rude ass too, baby."

"You wanna show me how much again?"

"I mean, I guess..." As she ducks beneath the covers and grants me my wish.

# Chapter 13

# Honey

*T**he next week*

...

"Thank you, Sweetheart, for indulging an old lady to-day. I've been looking forward to our lunch all week."

"Oh, Honey, you're welcome. And ma'am, old where? You are the youngest mama I know. I can only hope to look as beautiful as you when I, *if*, I reach your age." She rubs her hand along the interior trim of my truck, while gazing out of the window.

"This interior color is beautiful. How did the sales rep describe it?"

Pulling my brand new Santorini Black Range Rover SV up to the valet, I place it in park. I turn to Mila to respond to her in my best British accent imitating the sales concierge as he described the interior, "Mrs. Patrick, *this* is a natural light linear wenge veneer with mosaic marquetry. The perfect complement to the Santorini Black exterior."

We look at each other and fall out laughing while holding onto one another's hands. Basking in this moment, I silently thank God for Mila. Bleu not only found his forever, but he gave me a daughter. And according to Mila, he gave her a mom.

As the laughter dies down, I continue to hold onto her hand, "Mila. One second before we get out."

"Sure, is everything ok, Honey?"

"Listen, I know I may not be your biological mom, but I hope you look at me and will eventually learn to trust me as a mother figure. *Your* mother figure."

"Okay..."

"I can't tell you that I know what you are experiencing and feeling with regard to your Lupus diagnosis. And I want to be there for you anyway that I can, especially when you're not feeling your best. I've been researching it and I read how flare ups can be debilitating. That aside, I..." I take a deep breath because I don't want to overstep.

"I hear how you speak about yourself sometimes." She slightly pulls her hands away from me. I quickly explain, "I don't want to offend you or overstep. Please know everything I am saying is with love. Mila, I notice when you speak sometime, well, often, you speak as if your future is limited."

She rears back a bit. I hold onto her hands a little tighter. "Don't withdraw from me please."

"Now I see where your son gets it from," she mumbles but squeezes my hands and looks up at me with a gentle smile.

Returning the gesture, I continue, "Again, I can't even pretend to know what you're going through and how all of this affects you, but I am here for you if you let me."

Nodding her head, "What did I say to bring this conversation on? Or was this pre-planned?"

"No, it wasn't actually. The statement you made moments ago was, '*I can only hope to look as beautiful as you when I, **if**, I reach your age...*'"

She replied with a confused look on her face, "Right, I said I can only hope to look as beautiful as you when I reach your age."

"No, baby, you said *if* , **if** you reach my age, not *when*. And ya' girl is not old enough to be put out to pasture just yet." I wipe the tears from her beautiful face, "What that tells me is you subconsciously count yourself out. Like you're trying to prepare for an ending that you

may not experience for a century to come. Sweetpea, you have a LOT of life left in you, but I need you to **believe it** and **live** like you do. You are no longer alone, Mila. You have a gang of folks, a.k.a your new family, who will wreck some shit about you. Ya' hear?"

Laughing and wiping her face, she nods her head again. "May I hug you, Honey?"

"Girl, you better! I'm glad you beat me to it 'cause I was coming in hot!" I reach over and pull her into the tightest embrace that I can. I give her several moments to collect herself before I pull away.

"Alright beauty, check that gorgeous face of yours and let's take care of this errand really quickly before we head to lunch. I'm sure you are just as hungry as I am. Deal?"

"Yes ma'am." She refreshes her lipstick, touches up her hair, closes the mirror in the visor, allowing the valet to open her door.

"By the way, that red lip, chile, you trying to get someone killed." I giggle and walk around the vehicle and loop our arms as we walk into the Saint James Winery and Resort.

"I can't believe that I am now a part of this legacy." She looks around with wide eyes.

"Believe it, baby. Hello, Albert, is everything ready and to my liking?" I ask the maître d'.

"Yes, Mrs. Patrick, it is. Shall I lead you?"

"No thank you, dear, my daughter and I can manage."

"Of course, Mrs. Patrick, and good afternoon to you also, Mrs. Patrick." Albert turns his attention to Mila.

"Good afternoon, Albert. Nice to make your acquaintance."

This pathway is probably one of my favorite areas in the winery. As the kids say, *"issa whole vibe."* The soft, melodic smooth jazz pipes through the hallway. Just enough volume to catch your attention but not too much that its attention seeking. The soft subtle scents of sweet berries, a slight tang of peach and decadent cream flow through the air. It's heavenly, not at all overpowering.

The contrasting softness that creates an intimacy within a public area is evident in the sconces lined along terracotta walls. The flooring is made of large cobblestones where the click clacking of our heels reverberating through the hall is reminiscent of our heritage.

We slowly walk past the shoppes and through the restaurant into the tasting area, taking in the ambience, savoring the whispers of our ancestors. I look over at Mila. She appears to be transfixed and enthralled in this experience.

"First time here?"

"No, I've visited a few times, but this time seems...personal. Ancestral. It feels like history is humming in the walls. Gives me goosebumps and a high pitch ringing in my ears. Wow."

A soft smile graces my lips and I hug Mila's arm a little tighter, pulling her a bit closer to me as we continue our stroll. We travel the bend slightly and face a brightly lit area with two very tall and wide, rich, dark mahogany wood doors that meet a subtle arch at the top. The handles are as long as my arms, made of brushed gold that have delicate images of vines engraved in them.

There are two doormen who allow us entry into a private area without letting us break our stride.

"Oh, I've never-"

"SURPRISE!!!"

"Oh my God!" Mila shouts in surprise, pulling me behind her as if to shield me from harm. She turns and looks at me with wide, teary eyes.

"This... this is your errand?"

"No, sweetheart, this is your engagement party."

"Hey, Sweet." Bleu sidles up behind her, unlocking our arms so I can hand her off to him.

"Bleu? Bleu, what did you do, baby?"

Laughing, he tells her, "I'm giving you everything you deserve."

# Chapter 14
# Mila

The surprise and excitement I feel surrounding this engagement party is an understatement. I am pleasantly overwhelmed and so much more in love with JaCaryous and Honey. I'm sure my other people helped but *these two*... have cemented their way into my heart.

Bleu hugs me from behind and kisses my spot beneath my ear. "You happy, Sweet?"

"More than you'll ever know. How? When? And your mom is your true partner in crime."

"You know she loves her some Mila."

"You mean like *you* love you some Mila?"

"No one can match my love for you, Sweet."

"Aww, JaCaryous." I simper and place a teasing kiss on his lips. After a few seconds I attempt to move away before we get carried away.

"Unh Uh. Come here." He kisses me so passionately we forget there's a room filled with people. His grandparents included.

We hear a collective, "Get a room!!!" and immediately break out into laughter. Separating, I wipe his mouth of any remnants of me as he looks down at me adoringly. *I swear, I can't wait to have all his babies.* Startled,

I don't know where that thought came from...again.

Shaking my head, I step back and grab his hand. He directs us over to his parents and grandparents. They each hug and congratulate me, then Bleu. Stopping in front of Honey, I ask, "So no lunch today then?" We burst into a fit of giggles. Looking over at Bleu, he is so happy right now. I can literally feel the love pouring from him directly into my soul.

The afternoon was a wonderful affair. We ate. We drank. I met so many family members. We laughed. I cried. We received gifts. We heard stories and reminiscing of old memories. There was even some ancestral knowledge dropped. Bleu did his best to give me everything we did not do prior to getting married in Vegas.

Checking in with me, Bleu leans over, "How you doing? Need a little break?"

I nod my head.

"Cmon." He grabs my hand and we sift through the well-wishers until we sneak through a well-hidden door. He leads me down the cobblestone path to the wine cellar beneath Saint James Winery & Resort. It's cool, dark, and silent, save for the distant sounds of our celebration upstairs.

"This is not smart," I breathe, my back hitting the cool limestone wall, a chill running up my spine just as Bleu's hand trails down it.

"Neither is wearing that little ass dress outside like you ain't mine."

"Boy, don't start."

"Too late."

His mouth crashes against mine mid-retort, all tongue and hunger, *claiming*. I gasp, and that's all the space he needs. One hand cups my jaw while the other slides up my thigh, beneath my dress.

"Somebody could come down here," I whisper into his mouth, but my hips betray me, grinding against the growing pressure in his pants.

"Let 'em. They'll learn somethin'."

"You're so nasty, Bleu."

"You love it."

He hikes me up—*like I weigh nothing*—and plants me on top of a wine barrel. The hem of my dress bunches at my waist now, and his fingers are already pulling my panties aside like they offend him. He hums low and dark when he sees how ready I already am.

"Damn, Mi... this all me?"

"Shut up and—"

I don't get the words out before he sinks two fingers into me—slow, deep, like he's searching for my *soul*. My head hits the wall with a soft *thud* and a moan too loud for the location. He curls his fingers just right and feeling my legs shake around his waist like he's got me wired to voltage.

"You gon' make a mess in this man's winery," he mutters against my neck. "They gon' smell you in the damn Merlot."

"Then stop talkin' and *do somethin'*."

That flicks a switch.

He yanks his belt loose with one hand, not even bothering to get fully undressed. Just enough. Just what's needed. My nails dig into his shoulders as he lines himself up and slides into me slow-*too* slow-and then all

at once, hips pushing forward with zero patience.

"Oh my God—"

"Nah, baby. That's *your* man. Gat damn, Mi! You smell so fuckin good. You make me wanna devour your little ass."

The rhythm is relentless. Deep. Vicious. His hand over my mouth when I get too loud, but he's smiling through it, like hearing me fall apart on him is his favorite sound. I'm grabbing at his back, at his neck, at air, trying to ground myself as he takes me completely.

"Bleu... please."

"Please what?"

"Please... don't stop."

His grip tightens. "You think I brought you down here to stop?"

My release hits hard, shuddering through me, and he doesn't let up. Not even when I'm trembling in his hands. Not until he's spilling into me with a low, guttural growl against my neck.

We stay like that, panting, pressing together in the dark until we hear footsteps above them.

"Shit."

"Fix your hair," he smirks. "Your tongue gone get us caught."

"Like your stroke won't?" I question with a raised brow.

He grins, licking my bottom lip once more. "Worth it."

We straighten up enough to make it to the restroom for a more thorough cleaning then return to the festivities.

"Oh! There you two are!" Honey exclaims into the mic. And of course, all eyes swing in our direction. My face flushes red and Bleu chuckles, leading us to the front of the room.

"Come on, babies, say a few words." Honey beckons us.

"Thanks, Mama." Bleu kisses her on the cheek, removing the mic from her hand.

Honey steps down to sit next to Pops. I stand next to Bleu, hand in hand. As he thanks the crowd for coming and celebrating with us on our behalf, I scan the guests to find my people and of course they are front and center. Zariah, Redd, and Whyte are sitting together and standing near the door is Cara, who had to pop in especially for this occasion. She was in Europe somewhere earlier this week when we spoke. I grin and wave at her. She blows a kiss my way. Whyte's gaze immediately follows mine and he sees Cara. Her smile falters just a bit when she sees him but ever the calm, cool, and collected, she will not show her true emotions.

"Now for the surprise of the evening. Because I love love and am so very much in love with this beautiful lady," he squeezes me closer to him. "I want to gift someone in this room, the gift of love, a Cadence Kiss, if you will."

You can hear the crowd chattering with excitement.

"Ok, ok, if everyone would be so kind to remain in your seats. As you can see, the servers are giving everyone a box of Zoëra's exclusive pearlized truffle flight. Zoë come up here, cousin, and tell the folks about this delectable confection you are blessing them with tonight."

Embarrassed, Zoëra was escorted to the mic by who I could only assume was another cousin or brother. She quickly and quietly describes the beautiful treats she curated specifically for our event. Everyone ooo's and ahh's, offering thanks and generous applause before she scurries away to the back.

"Thanks, Zoë baby!" Bleu blew her a kiss, embarrassing her more. I smile because I know exactly how she feels in this moment. He turns to me, "Sweet, would you like to say something?" Narrowing my eyes, I take the mic from him.

Speaking softly, "Um, hey y'all." The crowd laughs, returning my greeting.

"I'm not the social one of the two of us, I'm sure you can tell. But I would like to extend my heartfelt thanks to each and every one of you. I'd like to recognize my crew: Cara, Zariah, Redd, and Weston. I love y'all beyond measure. Thank you for everything. And to my new

family, I love y'all real bad." We all laugh and they blow kisses my way.

"I am learning since living in Cadence that family doesn't have to share the same blood, but they can share the same heart. And that's what Honey, Nana, Sassy, Pops, JJ, Ace, and Boss do. They share my heart and

fill me with so much love, I don't remember how it feels to be alone in the world."

"To my Bleu. Man, listen." The crowd cheers and roars.

"You said all gas, baby, and I should have listened." I laugh heartily.

"I wouldn't change a moment of it. I love you, JaCaryous Kristoff Patrick, with everything in me. Thank you, baby, for loving me."

Before I could turn around good, Bleu grabs and dips me into a deep passionate kiss that makes me dizzy as he stands me up.

"Whew!" I yell into the mic. The crowd goes wild!

I wipe my lipstick off his mouth and hand him the mic.

"Aight, y'all. As you can see, it's time for me to get my girl outta here. So, without further ado... If everyone will look on the bottom of their box, the lucky winner will have a poodle etched into theirs."

"I won! I won!" a lady to the left yells, waving her box of truffles.

"Congrats! Ok! Ok! Settle down everyone! Let me tell you what you have won, young lady. You and three friends have won an all-expense paid trip to Ancestral Vines Winery, a Black owned vineyard on the west coast. I'm talking first class flights, luxury suites, the works.

Our good friend, Marcelle "Celly" Kendrick, is the sommelier there. And he will be hosting "A Blast From The Past" weekend. See me before you go for final details and congratulations again!"

"That concludes all the fun for tonight. We thank and love you all. Get home safe. Remember, if you really enjoyed the wine today and don't need to or can't drive, we have rooms and rides for you. No cost, no judgment." He turns the mic off, the music resumes, and he drags me to the dance floor.

# One Year Later, July 4th...

## *Thee Best Day of My Life*

Today, I finally get to marry *my* love, my human Book Bae, the man of my dreams, Mr. JaCaryous Kristoff *"Bleu"* Patrick. Well, marry him...again, this time I'll be 100% coherent AND have memories of the wedding and union, not some drunken ordeal on the Vegas strip.

And the weather today could not have been more perfect. A gentle breeze whisps across my face, carrying the delicate scents of coconut and vanilla. The sun is out, illuminating the day. It's bright but soft, not harsh like the Georgia sun that blisters in July. I feel my parents' spirit blessing me with a wedding day one only dreams about. My eyes mist at the thought of them no longer being on this earth. A thought I try my best to keep at bay.

I close my eyes, enjoying the feeling of the soft sun on my skin, careful not to overdo it. I don't want red, blotchy, butterfly shaped rashes on my face. Giving thanks and gratitude for the ability to experience the natural beauty of Aitutaki, a Polynesian island in the Cook slands. I begin reflecting on how I am standing right here today.

This past year has been a whirlwind to say the least, reflecting on how this time last year, I drunkenly married the love of my life. A soft giggle escapes my lips while recalling all of JaCaryous's shenanigans and expressions of love he has displayed. Even in the uncertain moments we both share, the love and commitment to one another eclipses all of that. What else would I expect from JaCaryous? He warned me, all gas, no brakes.

Bleu and his family have embraced me and empowered me and loved me beyond words. They make me feel love so deeply and completely, I no longer feel alone. I don't desire isolation. It's the opposite. I now crave the conversation and intimacy. Even the hugs and comfort from each one of them. The elders regale me with stories that seem to hum within me like a soft prayer and I am entranced, feeling as though I've been transported back in time with them.

JaCaryous made a promise to love me like the books I read. He hasn't disappointed me...at all. This wedding he has pulled together is a perfect example. This man watched me add pictures and colors to my Pinterest Board. He listened to me gush over a song or sentiment. In passing, I marveled at the colors of the lagoon that Aitutaki is known for and voilà, I am in the Cook Islands. I know absolutely nothing about Polynesia, besides a picture from the internet and yet, here I stand, marveling at my surroundings.

He has got to be exhausted. I feel like he's been on go, every day for the last year. The prep work alone should have taken a team to execute. Making sure my vaccinations are current. Making my hydration and rest a priority to reduce the risk of flare ups and fatigue. This man is nothing short of amazing. He is so Mila centered, i.e. Lupus conscious, he does things like on July 2nd, we hopped the Delta flight from Atlanta Hartsfield Jackson airport to LAX in Los Angeles. We left mid-morning to avoid the crack of dawn airport chaos that Atlanta's airport is known for having. He made sure we traveled first class to ensure proper space and to experience the perks that come with the first-class tickets.

This man made sure my carryon included all my meds, meal prepped snacks, and teabags. He added my favorite throw and was sure to spray it with L'Occitane's lavender spray. He remembered that I told him I do this when I travel because it helps calm me on the plane and sleep a little better in the hotel.

Upon our arrival in Los Angeles, we checked into the Presidential Suite at the Hyatt Regency Los Angeles International Airport. He bathed me, moisturized and massaged me, fed me, and made sure the room was pitch black with minimal sound. To say Bleu guaranteed the extensive travel would not bring me discomfort, would be an understatement.

The morning of July 3$^{rd}$, we boarded an early flight from LAX into Honolulu. We kicked it in the Delta Sky Lounge during most of our layover, which was a nice change. Everything was so smooth, no rushing and worrying. It was so nice having someone take care of everything for once, allowing him respite.

That same afternoon we left Honolulu and landed in Rarotonga International Airport then headed over to Aitutaki Lagoon Private Island Resort. It was more than I could ever dream of in my lifetime. He didn't tell me where we were going so imagine my surprise when I remembered briefly mentioning to Bleu how beautiful the lagoon looked and next thing I know, I am getting married here.

Hearing a rustling sound near me, I open my eyes.

"Hey, Sweet." He taps my thigh, "You got enough energy for dinner then catch our first sunset together in Cook Islands?"

"Anything you desire, love." I kiss his cheek and grab his hand.

We enter our beachside villa and a private chef is waiting with a refreshing drink and island style dinner. Listening to the waves crashing and the light scents of coconut and vanilla have me in such a relaxed state, I can barely keep my eyes open. Bleu has my feet in his lap, rubbing them and my legs.

He has pulled out all the stops. Anything I thought I may have wanted or needed to make this day happen, he has provided it for me. From the destination wedding, down to the delicate garter he says he can't wait to take off with his tongue. I asked him if he meant his teeth, he gives me his signature smoldering look and says, *"I said what I said, Sweet."* Then he winks and walks away. I can do nothing but shake my head because I literally had no words after that.

As crazy as this year has been for all of us, this vacation was very much needed. It's also bittersweet because this is the first year we are missing the annual July 4th celebrations in Cadence. It's a community staple, so the employees of the bar are tasked with hosting, the six of us just won't be there.

The most important thing he did was make sure our ceremony took place on July 4th, local time, keeping in theme with the birthdays, anniversaries, and holiday that fall on and are celebrated on this day. Cook Islands is in the South Pacific and is six hours behind Cadence.

With that in mind, Bleu mapped out the travel perfectly to ensure we arrive in the South Pacific July 3rd and will marry on July 4th.

We were also able to watch some of the celebration back home. That was cool because it lessened the disappointment of not being there. Everyone tried to assure me that they are where they want to be. But you know me, not wanting to put anyone out or make things difficult.

No one complained and we all had the same travel itinerary. I low-key think everyone might have appreciated the staggered travel schedule because this past week has been

brutal: making sure work was completed, arrangements were made and kept, facilitating the
 holiday events, and preparing for travel. I am praying for no flare up. I don't care if I have an IV hanging out of one arm while popping pills as I walk down the aisle. Nothing and no one is stopping me from marrying my Bleu.

\*\*\*

Bleu comes behind me and whispers, "Two celebrations. One day. A lifetime of love." Grinning, I kiss him soft and slow in response. He groans into my mouth, pulling himself away from me.
 "I've got to go, Mrs. P."
 "Wait! Bleu..."
 "Yeah?"
 "I... I..."
 His brows meet with a look of concern etched across his face. "Yeah, Mi?"
 "I love you, baby. Thank you," I say softly.
 He stands there for a second, looking into my eyes, surveying my person as if he was trying to convey his love with his eyes. "I love you too, Mila. What's going on in there?" He gently swipes his index finger over my temple.
 "I... I just wish your family and Boogie were here. I don't have any family and I'm feeling a little melancholy. After all, the ceremony was supposed to be a family affair that includes them. And before you say anything, I know Boogie is only a few months old but I miss my baby," I cry.
 "I don't know how I let you talk me into leaving him!"
 "Aww, baby, come here." I walk into his embrace. He hugs me hard for a few seconds and says, "You know I gotchu. Your man has taken care of everything, Mi. The

entire fam is meeting at the winery and they have a projector set up in the area we had our engagement party in so the fam can see everything. You'll be able to see Boogie then and anytime you FaceTime Mama, just to talk to him. I even have it set up where Honey,

Sassy, and Nana can interact with you while you're dressing and getting ready."

"Oh, JaCaryous," I whisper, my voice thick with emotion.

Bleu kisses my temple. "I told you, baby, just like the books you read." He winks.

I begin crying hard and so ugly. Bleu chuckles and wipes my tears.

"Hey, pretty girl. Cmon, stop crying, you don't want red eyes, red nose, and leaky boobs walking down the aisle, do you? Looking like you got into my stash."

"Boy!" I lightly nudge him away from me, laughing.

"There she is."

Squatting down to meet me eye level, "Baby, I love you more than life itself. I will move mountains for you. Have I not shown you that, Sweet? You act like *I* don't miss my mini-me. I would give anything to have him here celebrating with us. Along with Mama and them."

I nod my head. Thinking of the countless ways this man has done just that.

"And I'll continue to, Mi. It's my job to anticipate your needs and take care of them before you even know the need even arises. Feel me."

"Yes," I say weakly.

"Nuh uh. As loud as your lil short ass be, I know you got something better than that for a nigga."

"Yes! I feel you, Bleu," I yell, grinning from ear to ear.

"Bet. Keep that same energy when I get to *feelin' you* tonight." He winks, bending down again, this time to lick my lips.

"You so nasty."

"Only for and with you, Sweet."

Making me blush, I smile softly at him as he leaves out of the door.

It's so hard to believe how we met a year ago and within a week, this man had my heart, my mind, my body, sweet Lord he had my body, and my soul. He pulled the true Mila out of hiding, dusted me off, and has me shining like the diamond I am. How can I not love him?

## Chapter 15

# BLEU

Quickly walking away from the door, I dodge another bullet from my inquisitive yet discerning wife. I have been meticulously planning this wedding for her for the past year. We are in the Cook Islands, courtesy of my extraordinary wife. This woman never ceases to amaze me. From her design talents to her strengths to her exquisite tastes. She craves bespoke experiences, no matter the size, and I aim to please.

As the ancestors would have it, on April 13th of this year, Mila blessed me with my *literal* mini-me. Six pounds, nine ounces, 21 inches long, blue eyes, honey complexion, head full of beautiful brown curls. JaCaryous

JaMil Patrick aka Boogie. We were celebrating Redd and Zariah's pregnancy news, only to be given our own a month or so later. The girls were elated being pregnant together. Only Zariah delivered Novah, a beautiful baby girl, on her due date and Mila delivered Boogie a little over a month early on the same day.

Removing my ringing phone from my pocket, "Whassup, Honey?"

"Hey baby, checking in. Everyone is present and accounted for while staying out of dodge until the ceremony."

I chuckle softly, "I know I can count on you to keep things in order. Mi is going to lose it when she sees y'all, especially Boogie. She misses him terribly. Hell, we both do but she really does, to the point of tears. How is he? Y'all got enough milk? The video set up complete? Backdrop in place?"

"Sir, calm down. This is not my first rodeo. That baby wants for nothing. The video and everything is in place and ready to go. I hate we will not be present to help her dress but I'll take this small loss in exchange for the huge win for her. And I'll remember to FaceTime so she doesn't suspect anything. We just gotta keep that little one quiet." She chuckles.

"Man, listen. Small and loud just like his mama." I laugh with her.

"Alright, as y'all say, not too much on my people now."

"Ha! Thanks for everything, Ma. It's taking everything in me not to ruin the surprise. She's feeling a little sad missing family. But!" I exclaim. "When I pull this off for her, it will categorically go down in her lifetime of memories as thee best day of her life." I smile so big at the thought, I am showing every tooth in my head.

Mila brings out this side of me. I said it before and I will continue to say it, I live to make her life easier. Her strength is commendable but crippling at times. A woman like Mila deserves love and protection and for her person to support and empower her. Silently encouraging her to shine, on her own terms behind the scenes.

"I'm heading to your side of the resort to kiss my little man, then to dress for the ceremony. See you in a bit."

"Kisses." Honey replies and hangs up.

\*\*\*

The sun is slowly beginning its late afternoon descent, illuminating the sky but not scorching the earth. I was thankful for that since the ceremony is outdoors and I was in a long sleeve, blue linen suit heading

toward the altar. The things I do for my wife. The entire wedding party was a juxtaposition in perfect harmony. Just as she described: The various shades of cream, blue, and orange is the theme for her special day.

Garb ranging from linen suits and sarongs to the flowing ice blue material of my heartbeat's dress sweeping the alabaster color sand.

My heart is full while taking everything in. I can't wait for Mi to see it. She is going to flip! She's having a difficult time as it is controlling her emotions and tears. Before coming down to the shore front, I go to the

bungalow Mi is in, honoring her wish not to be seen before the ceremony, we each stand on either side of the door, her left hand in my right, the faint sounds of *"The Prayer"* song by Donnie McClurkin & Yolanda

Adams playing in the background. The moment the strings began playing, she cries out softly, "Oh my God, baby." And I hear the sniffles. They turn into full on sobs as I sing the prayer of this song to her. I finish it up with my own prayer, speaking life into her, our children, myself, and our marriage. I kiss the back of her hand and tell her to meet me at the altar.

I take a minute to collect myself once the door closes all the way. It feels like the weight of this past year is choosing now to release through my leaky eyes. I welcome it, it's been a long time coming. I clean my face with my handkerchief and head on my way to change my clothes and down to the beach.

A short time later, I am taken aback at how beautiful this has come together. The setting looks like a picture. The sand looks and feels so incredibly soft beneath my feet. It's golden hour just like she wanted.

A simple yet stunning bamboo altar stands at the water's edge, framed by soft white sheer drapes tied loosely with floral accents.

A white fabric aisle runner stretches down the center of the sandy aisle, dusted with scattered seashells and natural beach stones, like nature's own confetti blessing each step. Along the sides, large cylindrical
candleholders and votives glow with a soft flickering light, nestled in the sand and surrounded by smooth white shells, creating a glowing runway of warmth and invitation.

Wooden chairs with crisp white cushions form two neat rows on either side, simple and elegant, allowing the natural beauty of the beach to take center stage. The backs are adorned subtly with white fabric or
ribbon, catching the breeze just enough to dance slightly.

In the distance, soft waves whisper against the shore, creating a calming rhythm that underlines the stillness of the moment.

The sun filters through the drapes, creating a glowing backdrop that looks like heaven cracking open just for this moment. The warmth of the sand, the scent of salt in the air, the faint floral notes on the breeze.

I hold a sleeping Boogie while I greet and hug everyone else, then make my way to the altar. Softly in the background I hear our wedding song from Vegas, Louis York & Anthony Hamilton's *"Alone A Lot."* A faint smile plays across my lips. I reach up to discreetly wipe a tear from my eye.

"Heyyyy." I hear the soft lilt of Honey's voice. "Not anymore, baby boy." She puts her arms around me and lets me cry it out once again.

"I don't know why I am so damn emotional, Mama," I say, wiping my face, again. Nodding my head to the beat of the chorus.

She doesn't say anything, but she doesn't let me go either. Instead, she slides tissue into my hand to clean my face. I have the slightest regret of doing this a year ago without my family just as the track changes and

Chris Brown and Jordin Sparks sing about not having air. Man, if that don't sum up how I feel without Mi.

Straightening up, I collect myself, handing Boogie to my mama. I stand tall when I feel Pops, Boss, Ace, and JJ embrace me in a circle. The words of the song fade away while Ace gathers us in a quick prayer. The older men take turns kissing my head, JJ daps me up, releasing me to Nana and Sassy. They take turns fussing over me, speaking positive words over me then kissing and wiping my cheeks.

Ace takes his place at the altar, preparing to officiate the ceremony. JJ makes his way to stand behind me as my best man. The track changes again while Usher croons, *"Here I Stand,"* signaling the beginning of the wedding march. JJ claps me on the shoulder, "You ready?" I nod my head *yes*, not trusting myself to speak. Rustling behind me lets me know he is walking away to take his place beside Cara to accompany her down the aisle.

Briefly closing my eyes, readying myself, I exhale deeply and look up the aisle to see Zi and Redd coming down first. Zi is in a soft looking, barely there, peach color, flowing off the shoulder maxi dress, holding a single peach calla lily bouquet intertwined with pearls. Light aquamarine blue studs in her ears with matching bracelet adorning her wrist. The exact match and color that Mila wants. And my boy is in a cream color, short sleeve button down linen shirt and pants with black and deep aquamarine blue beaded bracelet adorning his wrist. A gold chain around his neck and chocolate diamonds in his ears.

Next is Cara and JJ heading down the aisle. Leave it to my girl to spice her dress up. I laugh to myself. Her dress is similar to Zariah's except she has cut outs on each side along her rib cage and a split along one leg.

I'm not even mad at her. She made sure that it is a tasteful design and I would not expect any less.

There's a beat between Usher and an instrumental I know all too well, the sound of Kenny G's *"The Wedding Song."* A hush comes over the small crowd when Mila appears at the entrance with Whyte on her arm.

Mila believes my family would only attend virtually and my dad would not be present to walk her down the aisle. The next best person is Whyte. I don't want her walking alone, she deserves better than that. She deserves to walk down the aisle and be given away by someone who knows and trusts her decision and me to be the man she needs.

Our eyes meet and the tears instantly pour from her eyes as she sees *our* family standing, Honey with Boogie in her arms, waiting for her to walk down the aisle. She lets out an audible whimper when she notices my dad as he bends to kiss her forehead and take her other arm. She has not one but two protectors escorting her now.

She looks like a sun kissed angel floating toward me. Her dress was designed specifically for her. It's an ice blue strapless ballgown with a full skirt, hiding her post-partum body; she was afraid would not fit into her dress. My God, she's so elegant and graceful, like she's walking on air.

The bodice is a plunging sweetheart neckline, sittin' 'nem titties up just right. I lick my lips thinking of all the ways I am going to enjoy her perfect body tonight. Her collarbone and shoulders are the perfect shade of burnt honey. The sun catches the encrusted tiny pearls and crystal beading, highlighting the dense cluster at the top and gradually scattering downward in an ombré effect. It hugs her torso like a second skin, giving elegance with a hint of sensuality. Her thick, luscious frame that she often worries is unattractive is one of the most beautiful bodies I have ever seen.

I'm really feelin' the *"exquisite"* beadwork, her words, not mine, the designer suggested she scatter throughout the skirt, each step causes the gown to catch the gentle breeze we're blessed with and shimmer, hips swaying like a pendulum, causing my eyes to follow hypnotized.

Her makeup gives a natural glow. Her hair is braided and piled atop her head with tiny pearl accents placed throughout. In her ears are sapphire blue studs, matching that sexy ass tongue ring that peeks out when she licks her lips. Around her neck is a tear drop shaped pearl. A gift from my parents. She didn't want a new or different ring so she's just wearing the band right now.

Finishing her look with the bouquet that ties it all together like she said it would. She was very specific in requesting a blend of peach, pale blush, creamy ivory, and soft periwinkle blue. Peach English garden roses,

Ivory and blush roses. Light blue forget-me-nots, White anemone with sapphires placed in the center, Baby's breath and pearls woven in between. And a small photo of her parents in a charm, attached to the stems.

A small gift from me to her.

I sound like a wedding planner as I check off each detail that I know my wife wants. For the last year, I ate, slept, and memorized literally every detail of this wedding to ensure she has the perfect ceremony since I robbed her of it last year.

She has made it to me when I hear Ace asking in his booming voice, "Who presents this woman to be married?"

Pops and Whyte say in unison, "We do." Just then, Boogie lets out a small yelp, causing everyone to laugh. Dad kisses her on the cheek and returns to his seat. Whyte dabs at Mila's eyes, whispers something in her ear, she nods her head, and he places her hand in mine. And I finally feel like all is right in my world again.

We stare into one another's eyes for a few seconds.

"Hey, Sweet."

"Hey, baby." She giggles. I exhale and we turn to face Ace just as *The Wedding Song* ends, timing the beginning of our forever perfectly.

# Chapter 16
# Mila

"You may now kiss your bride." I hear Ace say and I squeal when Bleu dips me and kisses me with so much passion, I can't catch my breath.

"May I re-introduce to you, Mr. and Mrs. JaCaryous and Mila Patrick!" Ace yells.

The crowd claps and screams, "Happy Anniversary!" Confetti falls from somewhere in the sky and the music volume increases.

I won't let Bleu go, making it difficult to hug everyone. Bleu and I walk over to Ace, where I hug his neck, thanking him for officiating. Then I make my way to the parentals and my son, taking a few moments to love and kiss on him. God, it's been a long few days without him.

"I thought y'all couldn't come, I've been crying all day. Now that I think about it, every time I would ask Bleu anything, he would distract me and evade my questions." His arms circle my waist.

"Mi, do you think I would honestly let my mama and grannies miss this? Or better yet, have YOU miss them being here?"

I blush, not answering his questions. "You're right. I was so in my feelings, I couldn't think straight. When I saw Pops at the top of the aisle, Whyte had to hold me up, I almost fainted." We all laugh at my antics.

"Aight, y'all, not to break up this happy moment but time is not ours today, we gotta get these photos before sunset. And then dinner, 'cause my stomach is touching my back!" He shouts.

"And I need to pump, baby."

"I gotchu."

Assembling to the designated picture spot, my goodness these photos are spectacular. Bleu literally thought of everything. I look over at my baby and even though he is beyond ecstatic, I can see the exhaustion creeping in. I make a mental note to take extra care in catering him tonight. He has made my every wish and dream come true with this wedding trip.

Shortly after dinner, I went up with Honey, Nana, and Sassy to nurse Boogie and change clothes. The rest of the night, beneath the glow of a thousand stars, we laugh, eat, dance, and they drink and smoke. Relaxing beside Bleu, his cousins from the winery, JJ, and our crew are chilling around the fire pit when someone turns on, "*Loves Gonna Last*" by Ray Silkman. The beat drops, I whip my head around and my eyes meet hers.

Cara's grinning, nodding her head, extending her hand to me, beckoning me to dance with her on the makeshift dance floor. I'm in my element now, reminiscing how my daddy first taught me to step. Like *for real* step, the Chicago way. My eyes close as I relive the memories while stepping without missing a beat. I know the exact moment when she hands me off to Bleu and to my surprise, my baby is almost as good as me. I know we have practiced a bit over the last year but not like this. My eyes widen and he's grinning hard but groovin' harder.

"Ok, baby, let's go then!" I shout, egging him on.

He's twisting and turning, walking and dipping me. I swear... This. Man. Right. Here. Nothing makes me happier than some of my favorite memories of back home, especially when my parents were alive. Leave it to him and Cara to make sure this was part of the wedding celebration.

Just as the song is ending, The Temptations "*The Jones*" mixes in. Bleu hands me off to Whyte. I'm winded but keep going. I don't want this fun to end. Al Wilson's *"Show & Tell"* is next in rotation. The elders have gotten on the floor, doing their two steps. Cara and I taught Whyte years ago how to step. He's an expert now. He and I fall into a familiar rhythm and cadence somewhat different from Bleu and me. He anticipates my steps and leads with ease. I don't know how long that song is but after about three or four minutes, I tap out.

"You look good out there, Sweet." Bleu wipes the sweat from my face.

"Thanks, Babe." I kiss his lips and lean on him. "Soooo..."

"Cara, nosy." He laughs because he was waiting on my question.

Laughing because I'm so predictable, "When though? Y'all sneaking around behind my back?"

"Girl, most of the time, it was right beneath your nose. Think back over the past year at how many "impromptu" get togethers or events we've attended and ended up dancing. That was *intentional*, ma'am."

"You are so sneaky, Mr. Patrick."

"Strategic, Mrs. Patrick. When you have a wife like mine, you have to be."

"Duly noted." I wink at him.

"Baby," I turn and look at him. "You are operating on fumes. I want to take care of you tonight."

"Shiiiittttt! Aight, y'all, me and the missus are out. Thanks for coming and shit but we will see y'all for breakfast in the morning." He finishes the sentence while pulling me behind him halfway down the trail back to the bungalow. All you hear is laughing and catcalling behind us.

***

Once in the room, I go into the bathroom, adjust the lighting, light candles, and start my playlist, I turn the water on in the shower to the temperature he likes. I look behind me and he's standing in the doorway watching me. I begin undressing. He begins unbuttoning his shirt. I walk over to him, removing his hands so I can do it instead. I stand on my tiptoes to kiss his collarbone and chest. He lets out a soft moan. I unbuckle his belt, remove it, his pants, and boxer briefs. Carefully maneuvering the clothing over his extremely hard dick.

"Sweet," he whispers my name.

"I gotchu, Babe. Let me take care of you tonight." Slowly swiping the pre-cum across the head of his dick with my thumb, he inhales sharply and shudders. I sink to my knees, hearing him groan.

I place the head of his dick in my mouth and suck on it. Swirling my tongue in a circular motion, I pull back, licking the head just like he likes.

"Ahh, Sweet, damn."

Deep throating him, "Mmm hmm." I allow the vibrations of my voice reverberate through him, eliciting a low moan, causing his knees to buckle. Gently pushing him back against the wall to support him, I continue summoning his ancestors with my talents.

"Mi, wait, Sweet."

I don't stop until all his little Bleus and Milas are gallivanting down my throat to their happy place.

I slide my lips backwards off his dick, sounding like I'm savoring my favorite watermelon blow pop and sitting back on my heels, looking up at him with wide eyes. His chest heaving. He wipes his hand down his face.

"Yes, JaCaryous?"

"Don't look at me all innocent, knowing your demonic ass has snatched my soul."

I laugh at how serious he is trying to regain control.

Batting my eyes. "What I do? Come on, drama, let me wash you and get you to bed."

I grab his hand, leading him to the shower where I wash him from head to toe, nice and slow. I have to sit him on the bench to reach him properly since he's so tall.

When we are done, he brushes his teeth and comes to bed where I have everything set up to rub him down. I want to relax him so he can get a good night's sleep. I power his phone off and place it on the charger. I send out a group text thanking everyone, setting a brunch time between 11a and 1p tomorrow, and letting them know we are unreachable until that time. I send a separate text to Honey, checking on her and Boogie.

She replies, assuring me everything is fine and not to worry. Cara replies, giving options on our return flights via private air carrier. I tell her to choose and let us know tomorrow of our itinerary. I bid everyone a good night so I can focus on my love.

Looking down at him, his eyes are closed. I pour some of the warm oil and rub it between my hands before placing it on his skin. I gently knead his muscles, and he moans softly somewhere between ecstasy and exhaustion. I keep a slow, steady rhythm, working quietly. When I hear the soft snores coming from him, I gradually stop rubbing him, I go wash my hands and put everything away before saying my prayers.

Checking my phone one more time to make sure there are no urgent calls or texts, I look over at my love and kiss his lips lightly before getting in the bed.

Before I snuggle up to him, I find Bleu's Affirmation on my phone that I recorded for him. Turning the volume down low enough so not to wake him but enough for it to seep into his psyche, I hit play and my voice softly fills the room. Bleu stirs a bit hearing me speak, but I immediately snuggle closer, kissing his shoulder, and he settles back into sleep.

*Dear Husband.*

*Thank you. Thank you for being the amazing human that you are. In the world's eyes you may not be perfect but in my eyes, you're perfect for me.*

*Thank you for being the man that I not only want but need. You see me. And I want you to know that I see you, too.*

*I see how you mentally prepare for every task to make our lives flow easier. I see your stress and exhaustion, and you n ever complain. I see when you're weary and need respite. P lease know it is my honor and privilege to provide that for y ou, just as you do for me.*

*I hear the words you don't speak and love how you allow me to fill in the blanks with no questions asked.*

*You once told me all gas no brakes. Just know that's how I'm coming before, beside, and behind you. At all times.*

*I always say the hardest job in the word is to be a Black man. And you. Black man. Are worthy. You are loved. You ARE love.  You are not inferior, you are a king, **my** king. You are not alone. I will help carry the load.*

*You are the head and I will follow your lead. I just ask that you respect my position in the decisions you make. And I look forward to a lifetime of decisions to be made **with** you.*

*Thank you. Thank you for being my safe space and trusting me to be yours in return.*

*I curated this affirmation just for you, JaCaryous, to listen to every morning before you begin your day, so you feel the armor of protection surrounding you. And every night before you sleep, to remind you of the greatness you are. And any time in between whenever you need.*

*My love for you knows absolutely no bounds. Never forget that.  And speaking life into you, especially when you need it most, is my pleasure.*

*I love you, husband. I love you, friend. I love you, JaCaryous.*

# Act 3

# Chapter 17
# Mila

*S*ix years later....

    Reminiscing on my move to Cadence and how my life has changed, I am in awe how everything played out for me. Growing up on Chicago's Southside with Cara, who now spends more time overseas than she does at home, gave me my first real friend. Then we went off to college together and met Whyte, Zariah, and Redd. I wonder where I'd be today if I never visited Cadence with Zariah. I fell in love with the city of Cadence the first time I went home with Zariah for the holiday and knew instantly where I was residing after I graduated.

Whyte and I hit it off as soon as we met. He's always felt like family. I just wish he and Cara would get it together. Whatever *it* is.

Cara is keeping busy building a new business. She told me once that she ran into Anise in Milan. I didn't know who she was talking about until she described the drunk chick hanging all on Bleu in Vegas. She was still doing the same thing – just in Milan. Poor child.

Redd and Zi are still together and doing very well. Thinking back, they have been together since... I've never not known them together in some capacity. They now have three littles. Redd and Bleu take the kiddos on play-dates. It's a sight to see. Whyte tags along and is the God-father to them all. Bless his heart.

Whyte. Whyte's tattoo studio is "the spot" to get your ink done. He's huge in the tattoo world. Still no serious girlfriend and I often wonder if he's waiting on Cara. He'll never admit it though.

Honey, Pops, Sassy, Boss, Ace, and Nana are still moving and shaking things up in Cadence and loving on the grands. The cousins and winery are thriving. Coming up with new ideas all the time.

And JaCaryous and I have been going strong. Despite my lupus diagnosis, I'm doing well - better than I ever imagined I could be. Bleu is thriving, and Boogie is healthy and strong. Life has found its rhythm again, steady and sweet. So sweet, in fact, that our family of three became a family of four. Two, almost three years after Boogie was born, we welcomed a gorgeous baby girl, JaMila Jessinia Patrick, looking just like her damn daddy. She even has bluish, green eyes. I guess my genes weren't strong enough and contributed where they could. I was worried Boogie would have a hard time no longer being an only child. The only challenge he exhibited was not being able to pronounce her name correctly when she was born. He called her Jam instead, and somehow the name just... fit.

Because there's always music playing somewhere in our world - soft chords floating from the living room, a beat humming in the car, someone's always dancing. Someone's always singing. And now, both my little heartbeats carry nicknames born from the rhythm that built this family.

Since JaCaryous and I began this crazy adventure, he has fully moved all his operations to Cadence. He's scaled back tremendously to be hands on with the kids and is no doubt the best dad ever. I landed a huge client, and that project set me up financially where I expanded my team. It allows me to be more selective in the projects we accept and less hands on. Don't get me wrong, I love interior designing, but it can be physically challenging. Then add kids to the mix and bay-bee! Luckily, I have a very supportive husband and family to step in and help because entrepreneurship by itself is a beast.

I say that just as I hear something fall in the other room.

"Boogie and Jam!" I yell into the playroom from the kitchen.

"Ma'am?" They yell back in unison. Moments later, I hear little feet heading in my direction.

"Yes, Mama?" Jam asks while climbing into my lap where I'm seated at the kitchen table.

"Sweet, that wasn't me-"

"Little boy, give me those lips."

"Mom! What did I do?" He smirks, looking more like his daddy every day. That dimple making its appearance in his left cheek, the only thing I think he got from me.

"You just mannish! No one calls me Sweet but my husband." I grab at his little lips, pretending I'm going to twist them.

He giggles, trying to run away.

"What's mannish?" Jam asks, trying to make it make sense in her three-year-old brain.

"Your brother thinking he can get away with things when he can't." I eye him and oversimplify my response for her.

"Forget all of that, what was that noise?"

Pointing at each other, "It wasn't me." They say in unison.

"Ok, you know I don't repeat myself, so we can put away the toys, no outings, and how about a time out. Maybe it's nap time."

"Noooooo!" They scream and run back into the playroom to clean up whatever they knocked down.

Smiling to myself, this life I have is beyond my wildest dreams. The difference between *Now and Then* is simple...JaCaryous "Bleu" Kristoff Patrick.

### *The End*

# Family History

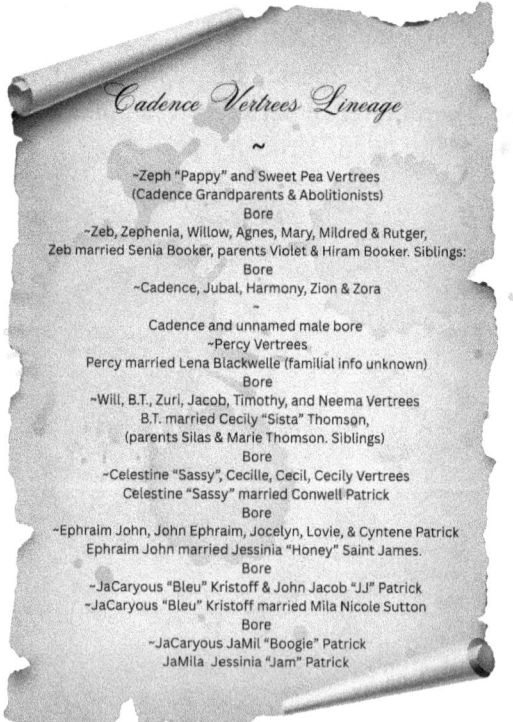

**Cadence Vertrees Lineage**

~

~Zeph "Pappy" and Sweet Pea Vertrees
(Cadence Grandparents & Abolitionists)
Bore
~Zeb, Zephenia, Willow, Agnes, Mary, Mildred & Rutger,
Zeb married Senia Booker, parents Violet & Hiram Booker. Siblings:
Bore
~Cadence, Jubal, Harmony, Zion & Zora

~

Cadence and unnamed male bore
~Percy Vertrees
Percy married Lena Blackwelle (familial info unknown)
Bore
~Will, B.T., Zuri, Jacob, Timothy, and Neema Vertrees
B.T. married Cecily "Sista" Thomson,
(parents Silas & Marie Thomson. Siblings)
Bore
~Celestine "Sassy", Cecille, Cecil, Cecily Vertrees
Celestine "Sassy" married Conwell Patrick
Bore
~Ephraim John, John Ephraim, Jocelyn, Lovie, & Cyntene Patrick
Ephraim John married Jessinia "Honey" Saint James.
Bore
~JaCaryous "Bleu" Kristoff & John Jacob "JJ" Patrick
~JaCaryous "Bleu" Kristoff married Mila Nicole Sutton
Bore
~JaCaryous JaMil "Boogie" Patrick
JaMila Jessinia "Jam" Patrick

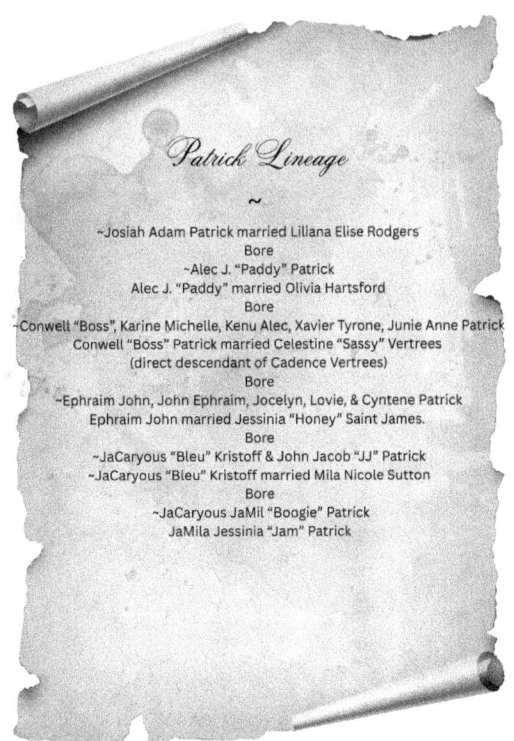

*Patrick Lineage*

~

~Josiah Adam Patrick married Liliana Elise Rodgers
Bore
~Alec J. "Paddy" Patrick
Alec J. "Paddy" married Olivia Hartsford
Bore
~Conwell "Boss", Karine Michelle, Kenu Alec, Xavier Tyrone, Junie Anne Patrick
Conwell "Boss" Patrick married Celestine "Sassy" Vertrees
(direct descendant of Cadence Vertrees)
Bore
~Ephraim John, John Ephraim, Jocelyn, Lovie, & Cyntene Patrick
Ephraim John married Jessinia "Honey" Saint James.
Bore
~JaCaryous "Bleu" Kristoff & John Jacob "JJ" Patrick
~JaCaryous "Bleu" Kristoff married Mila Nicole Sutton
Bore
~JaCaryous JaMil "Boogie" Patrick
JaMila Jessinia "Jam" Patrick

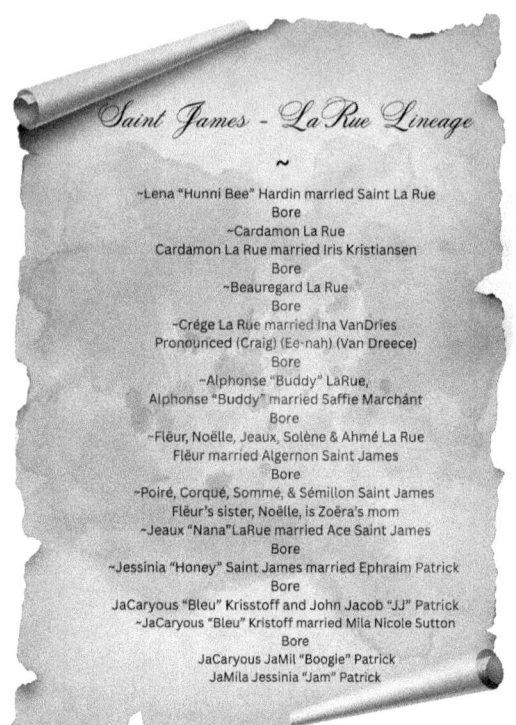

## Saint James - LaRue Lineage

~

~Lena "Hunni Bee" Hardin married Saint La Rue
Bore
~Cardamon La Rue
Cardamon La Rue married Iris Kristiansen
Bore
~Beauregard La Rue
Bore
~Crége La Rue married Ina VanDries
Pronounced (Craig) (Ee-nah) (Van Dreece)
Bore
~Alphonse "Buddy" LaRue,
Alphonse "Buddy" married Saffie Marchánt
Bore
~Flëur, Noëlle, Jeaux, Solène & Ahmé La Rue
Flëur married Algernon Saint James
Bore
~Poiré, Corqué, Sommé, & Sémillon Saint James
Flëur's sister, Noëlle, is Zoëra's mom
~Jeaux "Nana"LaRue married Ace Saint James
Bore
~Jessinia "Honey" Saint James married Ephraim Patrick
Bore
JaCaryous "Bleu" Krisstoff and John Jacob "JJ" Patrick
~JaCaryous "Bleu" Kristoff married Mila Nicole Sutton
Bore
JaCaryous JaMil "Boogie" Patrick
JaMila Jessinia "Jam" Patrick

## Saint James - La Rue Lineage
### cont.

~Isa Oebért married Mills Saint James
Bore
~James Saint James
James Saint James married Clea Louise Smith
Bore
~Ace & Algernon Saint James
Ace married Jeaux "Nana"La Rue
Bore
~Jessinia "Honey" Saint James
Jessinia "Honey" Saint James married Ephraim Patrick
Bore
~JaCaryous "Bleu" Krisstoff & John Jacob "JJ"Patrick
~JaCaryous "Bleu" Kristoff married Mila Nicole Sutton
Bore
~JaCaryous JaMil "Boogie" Patrick
JaMila Jessinia "Jam" Patrick

and
~Algernon Saint James married Fleur La Rue
Bore
~Poiré, Corqué, Sommé, & Sémillon Saint James

# Wineries, Pairings, & Such

## Black Owned Wineries worldwide

**McBride Sisters Wine Company** (USA & New Zealand) - Run by Robin & Andréa McBride, global footprint

**Brown Estate** (Napa Valley, USA) - First Black-family-owned estate in Napa

**Aslina Wines** (South Africa) Founded by Ntsiki Biyela, Black female winemaker

**Kumusha Wines** (South Africa / Zimbabwe region) - Founded by Tinashe Nyamudoka

**Lyons Wine** (Italy, Emilia-Romagna) - Chris Lyons making his mark in Italy

**Theopolis Vineyards** (USA, California) - Owned by Theodora Lee, Pasadena to premium Petite Sirah

**Vision Cellars** (USA, California) - Mac McDonald's brand, strong Black-owned name in fine wine

**La Fête Wine Co** (USA, Florida) – Donae Burston inspired by the Côtes de Provence Rosé

# ~Here's A Little Something For You~

*Cadence Kiss* is a Late Harvest Red, Sweet Syrah. While the wine itself is fictional, its profile mirrors real late-harvest reds that are berry-rich, velvety, and indulgently sweet. It pairs effortlessly with the Patricks' Sunday dinner menu: Herb-Seared Lamb Chops with Blackberry Demi-Glace, Crispy Rosemary Polenta Cakes, Charred Broccolini with Lemon Zest, and Fig & Honey Crème Brûlée with Fig Compote Garnish. Full recipes are included. A special highlight of the evening is *"**deCadence**"* Truffle Flight, curated by Zoëra of Saint James Winery.

# Herb-Seared Lamb Chops with Blackberry Demi-Glace

## Serves: 2–3 people

### Ingredients

- 6 lamb lollipop chops
- 2 tbsp olive oil
- 1 tbsp fresh rosemary, chopped
- 1 tbsp fresh thyme leaves
- 3 garlic cloves, minced
- ½ tsp smoked paprika
- Salt & cracked pepper

## Instructions

## Lamb Chops

1. Pat lamb chops dry. Season generously with salt, pepper, rosemary, thyme, garlic, and smoked paprika.

2. Heat a cast-iron skillet to medium-high. Add olive oil.

3. Sear lamb chops 2–3 minutes per side, until browned but still tender.

4. Rest 5 minutes before plating.

## Ingredients

## Blackberry Demi-Glace

- 1 cup beef stock

- ½ cup blackberry preserves or mashed fresh blackberries

- 1 tbsp balsamic vinegar

- 1 tsp Dijon mustard

- 1 tbsp butter

- Pinch of salt

## Instructions

## Blackberry Demi- Glace

1. Add beef stock to a small saucepan over medium heat.

2. Whisk in blackberry preserves, balsamic, and mustard.

3. Reduce 10–12 minutes until thickened.

4. Stir in butter for a velvety finish.

5. Spoon over lamb chops.

# Crispy Rosemary Polenta Cakes

## Ingredients

- 1 cup quick-cook polenta
- 3 cups chicken stock
- 1 tbsp butter
- ½ cup grated parmesan
- 1 tsp chopped rosemary
- Salt + pepper
- Olive oil for frying

## Instructions

1. Bring stock to a simmer. Whisk in polenta.

2. Cook until thick (2–3 minutes). Stir in butter, parmesan, rosemary, salt & pepper.

3. Spread into a flat baking dish and chill 30 minutes to set.

4. Cut into squares or circles.

5. Pan-sear in olive oil until golden and crispy.

# Charred Broccolini with Lemon Zest

## Ingredients

- 1 bunch broccolini
- 1 tbsp olive oil
- Salt & pepper
- Zest of ½ lemon

## Instructions

1. Toss broccolini in olive oil, salt, and pepper.
2. Grill or roast at 425°F for 10–12 minutes until charred at the edges.
3. Finish with fresh lemon zest.

# Fig & Honey Crème Brûlée

## Serves: 4–6

## Ingredients

- 2 cups heavy cream
- 4 egg yolks
- ½ cup sugar + extra for topping
- 1 tsp vanilla extract
- ¼ cup fig preserves or mashed figs
- 1 tbsp honey
- Pinch of salt

## Instructions

1. Preheat oven to 325°F.

2. Warm heavy cream in a saucepan until just steam-

ing.

3. In a bowl, whisk egg yolks, sugar, vanilla, honey, and fig preserves.

4. Slowly stream in the warm cream while whisking.

5. Strain mixture into ramekins.

6. Place ramekins in a baking dish; pour hot water halfway up the sides.

7. Bake 35–40 minutes, until centers are slightly jiggly.

8. Chill 2+ hours.

9. Before serving, sprinkle tops with sugar and torch to create the caramelized crust.

# Fig Compote Garnish

## Ingredients

- ½ cup chopped figs
- 1 tbsp honey
- 1 tbsp water
- Pinch of cinnamon

## Instructions

Simmer 5 minutes until glossy. Serve a teaspoon on top or beside the Brulé.

# "deCadence"

## Truffle Flight curated by Zoëra Saint James of Saint James Winery & Resort

### *Rosemary Honey Dark Chocolate Truffle*

Dark chocolate · honey · rosemary-infused cream

### Fig & Port Ganache Truffle

dried fig · port wine reduction · dark cocoa

### Blackberry Balsamic Dark Chocolate Truffle

blackberry purée · aged balsamic · 70% dark chocolate

### Smoked Sea Salt Caramel Truffle

caramel · smoked sea salt · semi-sweet chocolate

# Espresso & Cardamom Truffle

espresso · cardamom · bittersweet chocolate

# UPCOMING
# RELEASES

### *Cadence Kiss*

The Savored Velvet Collection Series

### *Blaque Orchid*

Fast & Serious Series

# Acknowledgements

My heart is so full right now and I pray I don't leave anyone out of my acknowledgement that should be mentioned. If I do, please blame it on my scattered mind and not my heart.

~Thank you, God, for giving me an outlet and opportunity to share my gift.

~Shouting out my babies, they are my biggest cheerleaders.

~Thing 2 & Thing 3 – Thank you for supporting, reading, and sharing.

~My Writing Crew – Twin, SA, & TMM, y'all make this writing thing better.

~My DF – Thank you, thank you, for always reading my texts, emails, & helping me make sense of the senseless.

~My Editor, V. Rena, thank you for righting my wrongs.

*Most importantly.... My Mom & Grandma  The two people who are solely responsible for my love of reading and my love of knowledge and adventure. Combined, my love for writing was inevitable.*

# Contact the Author

You can always check in with me via my website, Linktree or my socials:

https://www.theauthorcadencejames.com

**Linktree**: https://linktr.ee/theauthorcadencejames

**IG**: https://www.instagram.com/theauthorcadencej

**Facebook**: https://www.facebook.com/author.cadence.jame

If you or someone you know needs more information on Lupus, please contact the Lupus Foundation of America.

# Afterword

Whew... what. a. ride.

Bleu *did* warn us back in **Ignited On The Fourth** that he was "all gas, no brakes" when it came to Sweet, and y'all... he wasn't lying. I guess we finally saw what happens when a man keeps his promise *and* his foot on the pedal.

I shared at the very beginning that I wanted this finale in your hands much sooner, and life clearly had other plans. But my hope, truly, is that *Now & Then* gave you everything you waited for and a little extra on top.

If you haven't read **Ignited On The Fourth** yet, go ahead and fix that.

There are pieces of Bleu and Mila's journey tucked in those pages that make this book hit even deeper. Their love story is a two-part experience, and you deserve the full thing.

As always, I appreciate you more than you know.

If this book touched you, entertained you, or held you through a moment you needed an escape, please take a second to leave a rating and review. It helps indie authors like me more than words can say.

Thank you for reading, thank you for loving these characters with me, and thank you for believing in this world I'm building one story at a time.

See you soon,

**Cadence J.**

**xoxo**